FLASH

FICTION

FORWARD

FLASH FICTION FORWARD

80 VERY SHORT STORIES

EDITED BY

James Thomas and Robert Shapard

W. W. NORTON & COMPANY
NEW YORK   LONDON

Manufacturing by The Haddon Craftsmen, Inc.
Book design by Brooke Koven
Production manager: Amanda Morrison

Library of Congress Cataloging-in-Publication Data

Flash fiction forward : 80 very short stories /
edited by James Thomas and Robert Shapard. — 1st ed.
p. cm.
ISBN-13: 978-0-393-32802-8 (pbk.)
ISBN-10: 0-393-32802-3 (pbk.)
1. Short stories, American. I. Thomas, James, date.
II. Shapard, Robert, date.
PS648.S5F577 2006
813'.010806—dc22
2006009918

W. W. Norton & Company, Inc.
500 Fifth Avenue, New York, N.Y. 10110
www.wwnorton.com

W. W. Norton & Company Ltd.
Castle House, 75/76 Wells Street, London W1T 3QT

0

CONTENTS

CONTENTS

STORIES

John Edgar Wideman

for TH

A man walking in the rain eating a banana. Where is he coming from. Where is he going. Why is he eating a banana. How hard is the rain falling. Where did he get the banana. What is the banana's name. How fast is the man walking. Does he mind the rain. What does he have on his mind. Who is asking all these questions. Who is supposed to answer them. Why. Does it matter. How many questions about a man walking in the rain eating a banana are there. Is the previous question one of them or is it another kind of question, not about the man or the walking or the rain. If not, what's it a question about. Does each question raise another question. If so, what's the point. If not, what will the final question be. Does the man know any of the answers. Does he enjoy bananas. Walking in the rain. Can the man feel the weight of eyes on him, the weight of questions. Why does the banana's bright yellow seem the only color, the last possible color remaining in a gray world with a gray scrim of rain turning everything grayer. I know question after question after question. The only answer I know is this: all the stories I could make from this man walking in the rain eating a banana would be sad, unless I'm behind a window with you looking out at him.

EDITORS' NOTE

Flash fictions are everywhere now—on the radio, in magazines, on the Internet. When we began research for this book, determined to bring you the best flashes from America in the twenty-first century, we were gratified to see the growth of interest among writers, readers, students, and teachers after we introduced *Flash Fiction* more than a decade ago. We were amazed to see page after page of Google entries with competing "flash" definitions, contests, workshops, and conferences. It was so various we began to wonder again: What exactly *are* flash fictions?

Our conclusion, in the first *Flash Fiction*, was simply that they were *very* short stories. Granted, some of the stories seemed largely implied. Whatever they did—whether they evoked a mood or provoked the intellect, introduced us to people we were interested to

meet or described for us some unusual but understandable phenomena—most depended for their success not on their length but
on their depth, clarity of vision, and human significance. That was
all we needed to know. As editors we were open to almost anything. However, this time we had a score of readers around the
country helping us and we felt we needed more—a key, some
vital, crucial element about *flash*—to guide them.

First we looked to length. Our minimum from a decade ago
still seemed good. Not wanting to be too restrictive, we based this
on a question: How short can a story be and still truly be a story?
Some would say ideally as short as a sentence, but we found in
practice anything less than a third of a page is likely to be a mere
summary, or perhaps a joke. (In his book *Creative Nonfiction*,
Philip Gerard, in making legitimate a point about focusing any
writing project, tells his students every great book can be described
in a short sentence; they find this ridiculous and, challenging him,
ask, "What about *The Odyssey?*" to which he replies, "Guy comes
home from work.") For a maximum length, we kept to our original
750 words (the same as Hemingway's classic "A Very Short Story"),
which had a practical basis, too—to finish a flash fiction, you
shouldn't have to turn the page more than once. But nowadays this
may be problematic. What about radio? And e-zines, with scrolling
not only vertically but sometimes horizontally? Fortunately for us,
some of America's best writers have had something to say, not
about length but about the nature of very short fiction.

Richard Bausch, well known for his longer stories, added
another dimension after he took the challenge from *Five Points*
magazine to write a flash fiction (which you can find in this
anthology) and discovered that "when a story is compressed so
much, the matter of it tends to require more size: that is, in order
to make it work in so small a space its true subject must be pro-
portionately larger." This has two important implications, first that

the subject of a flash should not be small, or trivial, any more than it should for a poem, and second that the essence of a story (including its "true subject") exists not just in the amount of ink on the page—the length—but in the writer's mind, and subsequently the reader's. Charles Baxter takes this reader approach in his introduction to *Sudden Fiction International* when he refutes the idea that very short fiction has become popular because TV has dumbed us down. On the contrary, he says, readers process information much more quickly now (after all, this is the Information Age); many have become impatient with longer fiction because they're used to getting everything fast, almost all at once. Flash fiction, in other words, may be less about length than about us. Grace Paley seems to agree, linking readers to genre when she says, "A short story is closer to the poem than to the novel (I've said that a million times) and when it's very very short—1, 2, 2 1/2 pages—should be read like a poem. That is slowly. People who like to skip can't skip in a 3-page story."

This reminds us of a psychology experiment in which different genres of literature were used to test the different ways we remember things. It was found readers tended to remember individual words of poems, whether a few phrases or entire lines. But of course this wouldn't do for prose, trying to remember every word page after page—there were far too many. Instead, readers did retain a vast amount of detail by resorting to memory-organizing devices, ones familiar to us by traditional names such as character and plot. Thus we may allow an entire page in a novel to be forgettable, but we approach a flash fiction as if all of it may be memorable.

That was the key we were looking for, to guide those helping us gather works for this volume—a flash fiction *should be memorable*. Of course, there were other criteria—a good flash should move the reader emotionally or intellectually, it should be well written—and, not least, everyone had his or her own idea of what was uplifting, disgusting, hilarious, artful. . . . We hope readers of this book will find some of these stories memorable, too, and have as much pleasure in discovering them as we had in making the book.

THOSE WHO ARE truly a part of this book, not only by helping select the flash fiction, but in many other ways, are, first and foremost, Carol Houck Smith at W. W. Norton; Nat Sobel at Sobel Weber Associates in New York; Jesse Edell-Berlin, also in New York at Columbia; Jennifer Keeney Gantner, Jerome Gantner, Scott Geisel, and J. Andrew Root in Ohio; Margaret Bentley, Katherin Nolte, and Gwen Shapard in Texas; Tim Denevi, Angie Flaherty, Brent Fujinaka, Jess Kroll, Sarah Pardes, Janna Plant, Nani Ross, Leigh Saffold, Revé Shapard, and Sandi Yamada in Hawaii; Ian MacDonald in Arizona; John Soper in North Carolina; Mickey Edell in Michigan; and Julie Mason in Ontario.

James Thomas and Robert Shapard

FLASH

FICTION

FORWARD

JUMPER DOWN

Don Shea

Henry was our jumper up expert—had been for years. When the jumper was up, by which I mean when he or she was still on the building ledge or the bridge, Henry was superb at talking them down. Of all the paramedics I worked with, he had the touch.

When the call came in "jumper up," Henry always went, if he was working that shift. When the call was "jumper down," it didn't matter much which of us went—we were all equally capable of attending to the mess on the ground or fishing some dude out of the water.

The university hospital we worked out of got more than its share of jumpers of both varieties because of its proximity to the major bridges—Manhattan, Brooklyn, and Williamsburg. Over the years, dealing with his jumpers and the other deranged human flotsam the job threw his way, Henry got a tad crusty—you might even say burned out—although he was still pretty effective with the jumper ups. He always considered them a personal challenge.

Henry was retiring. On his last shift, we threw him a little party in the lounge two doors down from the ER, even brought some liquor in for the off-duty guys, although that was against the rules. Everyone was telling their favorite jumper stories for Henry's benefit; he'd heard them all before, but that didn't matter. Big John told the story of the window cleaner who took a dive four stories off his scaffolding. They got him in the bus, started a couple of IV lines, and John radioed ahead to the ER, "Bringing in the jumper down." Now this guy was in sad shape, two broken legs, femur poking through the skin, but he sits right up and says with great indignation, "I did *not* jump, goddamnit! I *fell!*"

Just as Big John finished this story, a call came in. Jumper up on the Brooklyn Bridge. Everyone agreed it was meant to be, it was Henry's last jumper, and I went along since it was my shift too.

The pillar on the Manhattan side of the Brooklyn Bridge is over water. Our jumper up had climbed the pillar on the Brooklyn side, which is over land. By the time we got there, the police had a couple of spotlights on him, and we could see him clearly, sitting on a beam about a hundred feet up, looking pretty relaxed. Henry took a megaphone and was preparing to climb up after him when the guy jumped.

It looked like a circus act. No exaggeration. Two half gainers and a backflip, and every second of it caught in the spotlights. The guy hit the ground about thirty yards from where we were standing, and Henry and I were over there on the run, although it was obvious he was beyond help.

He was dead, but he hadn't died yet. His eyes were open, and he looked somewhat surprised by what he had done to himself. Henry leaned in close and bellowed in his ear.

"I know you can hear me, 'cause hearing's the last thing to go. I just gotta tell ya, I wanted you to know, that jump was fucking *magnificent!*"

At first I considered Henry's parting shot pretty insensitive. Then I thought about it some. I mean, it was clearly not the occasion to *admonish* the jumper, who had obviously suffered enough defeats and rejections in his life. Why should he spend his last few seconds on this earth hearing how he blew it once again?

Seems to me if I was a jumper on the way out, right out there on the ragged edge of the big mystery, I might, indeed, upon my exit, find some last modicum of comfort in Henry's words, human words of recognition and congratulation.

THE MEMORY PRIEST OF THE CREECH PEOPLE

Paul Theroux

One person alone, always a man, serves as the memory for all the dates and names and events of the Creech, the hill-dwelling aboriginals of south-central Sumatra. This person possesses an entire history of the people and may spend as much as a week, day and night, reciting the various genealogies.

This Memory Priest reminds the Creech of who they are and what they have done. He is their entertainment and their historian, their memory and mind and imagination. He keeps the Creech amused and informed. The Creech have no chief or headman. The Memory Priest serves as the sole authority.

The Memory Priest is awarded his title at birth. As soon as he is able to talk he is given to understand that he is the repository of all the Creech lore.

His is not an easy career. He must memorize great lists of family names and must be able to recite all the events that took place from the moment of his birth.

The Creech are mostly placid, though they are subject to odd fits of violence. Biting themselves in order to show remorse is not unknown, and clawing their own faces is common. They are also untruthful and unreliable, prone to thieving, gossiping, gambling, and sudden spasms of the most aggressive behavior.

What the Memory Priest knows, the immensity of his storehouse of facts, is nothing compared with the one fact that he does not know, a secret that is withheld from him: After thirty years have passed, and he is old by Creech standards (possibly toothless, almost certainly wrinkled and shrunken), a meeting is convened. He recites the Creech history, and at the conclusion of this he is put to death. He is finally roasted and eaten by every member of the Creech, in a ritual known as the Ceremony of Purification.

The next male child born to a Creech woman is designated Memory Priest and elevated; history begins once again. Nothing that has taken place before his birth has any reality, all quarrels are settled, all debts nullified.

So the Memory Priest, now an infant, soon a man, learns his role, believing that history begins with him and never aware that at a specified moment his life will end. Yet it is the death of the Memory Priest that the Creech people live for and whisper about, the wiping out of all debts, all crimes, all shame and failure. They eagerly anticipate the amnesia his death will bring. Throughout his life, though he is unaware of it, he is less a supreme authority than a convenient receptacle into which all the ill-assorted details of the Creech are tossed. Secretly, he is mocked for not knowing that it will all end in oblivion, at the time of his certain death.

SASHIMI CASHMERE

Carolyn Forde

Two sushi chefs begin arranging their work under fluorescent lights. They lay the cold damp slabs of flesh in concentric circles, alternating from tongue pink tuna to opaque white squid. They are noiseless and efficient. Their hands move rapidly, hovering over their art. They are surgeons performing a delicate operation.

The spiral starts around her belly button. Her midriff is a checkerboard. They move to her upper body and cover her breasts with the round purple suction cups of octopus tentacles, her throat with green *shiso* leaves. Below her waist they place a small triangle of blowfish—poisonous if improperly prepared—where hair would have been. A brush with death is more thrilling and more costly when eaten off a foreign woman. Her legs are covered with California rolls. They place edible flowers in her navel, in her underarms, behind her ears and in her hair and even tuck one between her thighs. She is garnished.

She is rolled from the harshly lit kitchen into the dim light of the restaurant. As her eyes adjust to the darkness she sees only the ceiling, which is covered with pinprick halogen stars. She hears low male voices murmuring appreciation when she arrives at their table.

She feels small jabs as chopsticks lift pieces of fish from her chest, her shoulders, her ankles. She conjures the image of herself reflected in a gilded fitting room mirror. She is flawless in couture. She is immaculate in Armani. The air feels chilly as the men remove the cold pieces of fish one at a time, revealing damp patches of bare skin. Staring at the ceiling stars she imagines she is at the beach. She wishes she could smile but remains expressionless. The raw fish is a blanket. She wants to stretch, to move her legs, but has to wait for the party to finish. The sashimi becomes cashmere against her skin as she thinks of the Calvin Klein sweaterdress she will buy tomorrow.

The drunken chatter is easy to tune out because she can't understand it. The clicking and probing chopsticks are harder to ignore. One misses the blowfish entirely and slides where it shouldn't, another tries to lift her nipple as though it were a separate piece of edible meat. None of the men enter her field of vision, and, as far as she can tell, none try to see her face. She is a table, a plate with a pulse. These men are consuming the most expensive meal in the world. By the end, the artistic arrangement is left an abandoned and incomplete puzzle. A clap announces the end of the party. She is rolled away.

THE BARBIE BIRTHDAY

Alison Townsend

Girls learn how to be women not from their dolls
but from the women around them
—YONA ZELDIS McDONOUGH, *The Barbie Chronicles*

The first gift my father's girlfriend gave me was the Barbie I wanted. Not the original—blond, ponytailed Barbie in her zebra-striped swimsuit and matching cat-eye shades—but a bubble-cut brunette, her hair a color the box described as "Titian," a brownish-orange I've never seen since. But I didn't care. My hair was brown too. And Barbie was Barbie, the same impossible body when you stripped off her suit, peeling it down over those breasts without nipples, then pulling it back up again. Which was the whole point, of course.

There must have been a cake. And ten candles. And singing. But what I remember is how my future stepmother stepped from the car and into the house, her auburn curls bouncing in the early May light, her suit of fuchsia wool blooming like some exotic flower. Just that, then Barbie—whom I crept away with afterwards, stealing upstairs to play with her beneath a sunny window in what had been my parents' bedroom.

She likes me; she really likes me, I thought, recalling Shirley's smile when I opened the package. As I lifted the lid of Barbie's narrow, coffin-like box, she stared up at me, sloe-eyed, lids bruised blue, lashes caked thick with mascara, her mouth stuck in a pout both seductive and sullen. Alone, I turned her over and over in my hands, marveling at her stiff, shiny body—the torpedo breasts, the wasp waist, the tall-drink-of-water legs that didn't bend, and the feet on perpetual tiptoe, their arches crimped to fit her spike-heeled mules as she strutted across the sunny windowsill.

All Barbie had to do was glance back once and I followed, casting my lot with every girl on every block in America, signing on for life. She was who I wanted to be, though I couldn't have said that then, anymore than I could have said that Barbie was sex without sex. I don't think my stepmother-to-be knew that either, just that she wanted to please me, the eldest daughter who remembered too much and who had been too shy to visit. My mother had been dead five months, both her breasts cut off like raw meat. But I yearned for the doll she'd forbidden, as if Barbie could tell me what everything meant—how to be a woman when I was a girl with no mother, how to dress and talk, how to thank Shirley for the hard, plastic body that warmed when I touched it, leading me back to the world.

SWEET SIXTEEN

Gary D. Wilson

and never been kissed, she teases whenever she wants to be again, like now, like she's been doing all evening in my car in front of her house, the windows fogged over, Paul Anka crooning, her head on my shoulder, my left arm locked numb against the door, my right around her, aching vaguely, fingers tingling like they're asleep or frozen, sparks shooting through the ends of them inches above her right breast, but I dare not move or speak for fear I'll ruin everything, look totally stupid, like some twelve-year-old trying to get through a doorway without running into it and she'll wish she were with someone else, any one of at least a dozen other guys we both know would give anything to be where I am, doing what I am, her long brown hair smelling of shampoo and fallen leaves and tasting the way I think a girl's is supposed to as she finger-combs it back from her face and looks at me, eyes half closed, lips searching for mine, which they find, nipping, nibbling, joining, our breaths mingling, mine spilling over the soft bare expanse of her neck she suddenly tucks away—that tickles too much—and snuggles deep into the crook of my arm, a long breast-raising sigh that brings strands of mohair sweater to the tips of my fingers which she lifts just in time to kiss one after another, before holding them to her cheek—cold hand, warm heart—and guiding them back to rest, poised perfectly above the swell of her breast, which I know she wants me to touch in the way she— and I, I suppose—imagine a lover would, but she does nothing to make it happen—doesn't shift up against me, as if chilled, doesn't lay her hand on top of mine, pressing it gently down—and I do nothing, either, even though the tingle in my fingers has become almost painful again, and I know as sure as anything, without quite understanding why, that if not then, never, that once this moment is gone, it can't be recaptured, re-acted— although perhaps rethought, re-created—and that a time will arrive sooner than we can possibly anticipate when the porch light being turned on at her house will not mean her father thinks she should come in but that he's died, felled by a heart attack on his way out the door to retrieve the Sunday paper, and that his wife, her mother, will, in a fit of grief, move the family to be closer to her own in Colorado and we will lose contact long before it would have occurred naturally, and she will eventually marry and move to Hawaii, divorce and move to Seattle, where I will write her, asking how she is and will receive no answer, and I'll wonder for a long while whether she does, or ever has herself wondered.

BEFORE THE BATH

Ismail Kadaré

translated from the Albanian by Peter Constantine

He approached the tub of hot water, his eyes clouding with pleasure (how many times had he dreamt of this tub in his cold tent on the plains!), and just as he dipped one foot in the water he turned and looked at his wife, who was walking a few steps behind him. Her face still wore the flickering smile, but, even more than by the smile, his attention was caught by the metallic sheen of the object twinkling beneath the fabric his wife was carrying in her hands. Although his whole body was moving towards the bath, climbing into the tub, his curiosity still made him turn his head to see what the metallic object might be. (Perhaps during his long absence new utensils had been invented— even for bathing.) At that very moment he saw his wife almost above him, ready to cast the unfurled fabric over him ("What is this crazed woman doing?" he thought. "Who has ever heard of a man drying himself before a bath instead of after?"), and an instant later, before he was even seized by the terror of the thought that the fabric looked more like a net, he felt his arms entangled, and in the same instant saw the short axe in his wife's hands. The pain on the right side of his neck and the first spray of blood seemed to coincide with the shout of "Murder!" which he heard as if from the mouth of another.

He found himself outside the tub again, as if to amend an error, and, as before, he dipped one foot in the water, then saw his wife who was walking a few steps behind him, saw the flash of the axe beneath the fabric and, unable to make out what was happening, before he was even seized by the terror of the fabric turning into a net that bound his arms, he heard the first slash, and the blood reddened the water.

He found himself outside the tub again, as if to amend something, but this time slowly, as if he were coolly trying to resolve a misunderstanding. He approached the tub—the hot steam made everything seem more distant—his eyes clouding with pleasure (How many times had he dreamt of this tub in his cold army tent, when frantically, covered in grime, he had made love to a captive!), and just as he dipped one foot in the water he turned and looked at his wife, as if to assure himself that happiness was very near. Her face still wore that flickering smile, like a flickering, shifting mask, but, even more than by the smile, his attention was caught by the metallic sheen of the object twinkling coldly beneath the fabric his wife was carrying in her hands. And yet he thought as intensely of the love he would be making to her very soon as he thought that this metal—or rather hoped that this metal—had something to do with one of her surprises, those sudden and pleasurable surprises when he returned after long separations . . . At that very moment he saw his wife above him and the fabric turning into a net, his arms caught, the axe, the slash, the spray of blood, the cry of "Murder!" all happening in such quick succession that they intermingled and became one, until he found himself again outside the tub, moving towards her, found his wife walking a few steps behind him with the fabric in her hands, and this time the memory of the tent on the plains, his wife's mask-like smile, the flashing of the axe as it hit the water, all intermingled with lightning speed, making way for the slowness that was to follow. Before he saw his wife, he saw her shadow on the water, and then, when he saw her holding the unfurled fabric, he wanted to say to her "Darling, what is this new little trick of yours?" But it was just at this moment when the fabric took on a new guise, with nodes and nerves like those on the wings of bats, and the fabric slowly flew over his head, and the closer it came, the more clearly he saw that it was a net, and before he even felt his arms grow numb as it touched them, before the axe hit him in the neck, he said to himself "This is the end," and from the moment of this thought to the moment the blood reddened the water it seemed as if an interminable time had passed.

He found himself outside the tub again, moving towards her, as he had a million times before, experiencing with different rhythms this final fragment, these last twenty-two seconds of his life. This was the hell of Agamemnon of the House of Atreus, murdered by his wife on the first day of his return from the Plains of Troy, at thirteen hundred hours and twenty minutes, March 31, in the year eleven hundred and ninety-nine before our era.

BAKER'S HELPER

Cynthia Anderson

The girl who doesn't eat comes here to Jimmy's each day at the same time. You'll be filling a tray of cannoli, and there she is, crouched by the case, her face pressed against the glass. You mix sugar and ricotta, wipe your hands on your apron, all the while watching her.

She is thin, almost fleshless, her olive skin drawn tight against bone. Even so, kneeling there she's Botticelli-beautiful, with dark curls and a full mouth. You don't move as her eyes take in the racks of tiramisu and macaroon—revealing what she likes by where her gaze lingers. Sometimes her breath leaves puffs on the glass and you think *angel* but there are fingerprints too, faint whorls you find later when you Windex the glass.

Finally you ask "Can I help you, miss?" the way you would any-one, you hope.

Her eyes rise slowly. Your heart moves, resettles in a different place. "Just looking," she always says, her voice soft, as if she's down the street at Bova's browsing silver. Then she stands, step-ping back and running her tongue over dry lips.

You turn to another customer, conscious of Jimmy in the back. When you look again, the girl is gone, until tomorrow, when she will return as Jimmy is pulling biscotti from the oven and the bak-ery is filling with the nutty scent.

Daily the girl who doesn't eat is thinner but beautiful as you wait, watching, until one afternoon she struggles to rise from the case and you realize she is disappearing. You see ribs through her blouse, her clavicle, the bones of her jaw. That night you lie awake in the hot still air. When you do sleep, you dream of sparrows that gather on the stone steps of the park at lunchtime.

In the bakery the next morning you fill a box with things she likes, one sweet after another. You begin to feel better. You hum, licking chocolate from your fingers. That's right. You will feed the girl who doesn't eat.

You are ready when she comes, catching her before she kneels. "Here, miss," you say, sliding the box across the counter. "This is for you."

The girl stares at the string-tied package.

"It has everything you love," you tell her. "Lobster tails and babas, couple of half-moons. Take it, please." You push the box closer. Her fingers touch one side, yours the other.

The pulse at her neck throbs. "No," she says. "I can't. I—" She pulls back her hand, looks at you as if she's trapped. "This is a nice place," she says, then she is gone, the door banging closed behind her.

*   *   *

You HIDE THE BOX behind the cakes, and when you leave you take it with you. It's not good, stealing, but that night when you lie in bed letting one of the babas dissolve in your mouth, you realize all this really belongs to the girl who doesn't eat, not to Jimmy, anyway. She has earned it.

The next afternoon, the girl does not appear, which doesn't surprise you. You hate yourself, waiting, but she never shows up.

On the third night you're leaving Jimmy's after work when from the street you spot her inside Carducci's. The girl stands apart from the espresso drinkers, holding a basket of pizzelle. She brings the wafers to her nose, and you inhale anisette with her. You are dizzy, there on the dirty sidewalk, not knowing whose longing you are feeling, yours or hers.

You lean against the brick and light a cigarette, considering what you'll say when you go inside, practicing all the ways you won't ask how you can help.

RUMORS OF MYSELF

Steve Almond

In Nebraska I met a man, or possibly further north, and left him for his wife to find. His sedan drove well and I don't know honestly why I abandoned it outside Pierre—there was something in the air I liked, an apple stillness that reminded me of fall.

Daytona was nothing like I'd imagined. They drove slowly there, beaches stained yellow with rain. I met a waitress who showed good mileage. She seemed to agree with my habits and went easily along. I doubt a cigarette would have saved her but found I had to ask, her hips hung red with indecision.

In winter I circled the southwest, where truckstop lights showed scorpions scattered across the sand. A professor took me to bed among them, a sticky pile of pictures, his wife and children in his wallet.

Up north the rains blur everywhere and trees lend us the impression of a time less hindered by travel. A man with a reliable car found me coiled by the side of the road. I didn't ask for him to stop or to open his door. He told me of his years on the police force bopping niggers on the head and doted on a doberman he nursed himself by hand.

I stumbled down Mississippi looped in the loose arms of cloverleafs and sometimes slept against concrete. An insurance man in Beaumont funneled me pills as smooth as skin. He wanted to be trusted. He said I should lie still and wait till I felt the ocean.

My own mother never asked for an accounting of me. She knew love was nothing more than a failure to discern.

And so my young quarry, limp with sleep, I shall ignore the roadmap of peril tattooed along your belly. Let us lie here yet awhile and sift the radio for rumors of myself and, as the day turns tender, watch the clock of clouds blink red. The past will only keep swallowing the present, but often that's okay. Catch me on the right day and this car of yours becomes a painted bow and the gift of your faith plucks me inside. And I can assure you without hesitation that my fingers have never misunderstood flesh, not once, have arrived in the province of death at the invitation of sorrow.

There is no sorrow in your dreams my dear girl, my dear sweet young girl. And so I am incapable of harm. I am blameless, translucent.

MANDELA WAS LATE

Peter Mehlman

Mandela was late. Frankly, as a parole officer, you root for your thugs to come late or, better yet, not show at all. They get kicked back in the can where they belong, and you have time for a sandwich. But somehow, I felt different about Nelson Mandela. Maybe I was losing my edge, but he seemed somehow more respectable than most of the ex-cons who pollute my schedule.

In twelve-plus years, the only time Mandela missed a meeting was when he got a Medal of Freedom or some shit from some panel of European gasbags. Personally, I don't think getting sprung from the joint should get you any medals, but Mandela gave me eight months' notice and politely asked if we could reschedule. Thinking the bogus award might give him some positive rein-forcement, I let him slide.

Clearly, I set a bad precedent, because now it was 11:03 A.M. and he was AWOL for his last meeting. I considered Mandela among the top fifteen most effective rehab jobs I'd ever done, but let's face it, you can't argue with statistics. The recidivism rate for a guy who does twenty-seven years in the clink is up there with the chances of your Beemer getting jacked in Johannesburg.

Jacking Beemers. *If that's what Mandela's up to, I swear I'll run that self-destructive son of a—*

My door swung open. It was Mandela. It took every muscle in my neck to keep from looking at my watch. Instead, I went through my routine, taking in his overall mien: blue blazer, white shirt, plum tie, gray "ANC Athletic Dept." sweatpants. Right off, the flashiness of the tie queered me. Maybe his ex-wife was back in the picture. What was her name?

I peeked at the file on my desk labeled MANDELA, NELSON (GUERRILLA/#20742-0019) and saw her name: Winnie. Right. My old colleague Briscoe was her PO. One day he went out on his lunch break to get his negative HIV results framed under glass and was found with a pickax in his head.

Phrases like "material breach" and "consorting with known criminals" flooded my head. I stepped toward Mandela and frisked him: hankie, debit card, two-way pager, signed photo of Gwen Stefani, and the keys to every city on earth with a mayor. I moved on. Subtly, I smelled his breath. A hint of scrambled egg whites, but nothing to raise any red flags. Mandela was clean. Still, my antenna was up. Way up.

"Have a seat, Nellie."

He lowered himself into a chair slowly, like Gandhi ten days into one of his crash diets.

"Rough night? You seem a little stiff."

"I'm eighty-four years old," said Mandela.

Of course. Every hood walking through my door thinks he's the victim.

"What have you been up to?"

"Today?"

"Today, yesterday, Tuesday. Whatever. Start with today."

"I had scrambled egg whites with Kofi Annan, a conference call with Colin Powell, and posed for Richard Avedon."

Annan, Powell, Avedon. I made a note to run the names.

"But are you keeping busy?"

Mandela rolled his eyes. Oh, great, I thought. Here we go.

"Well, the press picked up on a talk I gave in which I referred to George W. Bush as 'a president who has no foresight, who cannot think properly.'"

I bolted up. "I knew it! The same crap that got you in trouble last time."

"Yes," he said with cool defiance, "but now we live in a free country."

"Not for repeat offenders, it's not!"

Mandela threw me a facial expression I couldn't have read with an X-ray machine. Truth is, I'd forgotten about the whole "free country" thing. It took me twenty-five years to learn that the *h* in *apartheid* was silent, and by then the game was over. Mandela was right. Legally, I had no beef with him. That's my problem with cons like Mandela: They make me feel really unintelligent.

For ten seconds, Mandela and I didn't say a word. Luckily, I had time: My noon appointment had to cancel after being shot to death on his way to picking up a new bulletproof Mercedes. Suddenly, I realized that irony was everywhere, and this whole charade was just a charade. Maybe Mandela would go straight, or maybe he'd backslide into the sludge of human rights. The fact is, people do what they do, whereas fish are driven mainly by instinct.

I cleared my throat and broke the silence.

"Hey. That Hugh Masekela can really blow the crap out of a horn, huh?"

I caught him off guard with that one. Mandela's face softened. He looked like he wanted to smile or become violently ill. Or maybe he'd split the difference and become nonviolently ill.

"Look, Nelson, we're done together. I'm ending your parole. You're free."

Mandela joyfully looked up and said, "Good. I was going to make some calls and have you fired anyway."

"Well, then, we've found some 'common ground,' as you would put it."

At that, Nelson Mandela stood up, walked out, and I never saw him again.

But then, it's only been three weeks.

SLEEPING

Katharine Weber

She would not have to change a diaper, they said. In fact, she would not have to do anything at all. Mrs. Winter said that Charles would not wake while she and Mr. Winter were out at the movies. He was a very sound sleeper, she said. No need to have a bottle for him or anything. Before the Winters left they said absolutely please not to look in on the sleeping baby because the door squeaked too loudly.

Harriet had never held a baby, except for one brief moment, when she was about six, when Mrs. Antler next door had surprisingly bestowed on her the tight little bundle that was their new baby, Andrea. Harriet had sat very still and her arm had begun to ache from the tension by the time Mrs. Antler took back her baby. Andy was now a plump seven-year-old, older than Harriet had been when she held her that day.

After two hours of reading all of the boring mail piled neatly on a desk in the bedroom and looking through a depressing wedding album filled with photographs of dressed-up people in desperate need of orthodonture (Harriet had just ended two years in braces and was very conscious of malocclusion issues) while flipping channels on their television, Harriet turned the knob on the baby's door very tentatively, but it seemed locked. She didn't dare turn the knob with more pressure because what if she made a noise and woke him and he started to cry?

She stood outside the door and tried to hear the sound of a baby breathing but she couldn't hear anything through the door except the sound of the occasional car that passed by on the street outside. She wondered what Charles looked like. She wasn't even sure how old he was. Why had she agreed to baby-sit when Mr. Winter approached her at the swim club? She had never seen him before, and it was flattering that he took her for being capable, as if just being a girl her age automatically qualified her as a baby-sitter.

By the time the Winters came home, Harriet had eaten most of the M&M's in the glass bowl on their coffee table: first all the blue ones, then the red ones, then all the green ones, and so on, leaving, in the end, only the yellow.

They gave her too much money and didn't ask her about anything. Mrs. Winter seemed to be waiting for her to leave before checking on the baby. Mr. Winter drove her home in silence. When they reached her house he said, My wife. He hesitated, then he said, You understand, don't you? and Harriet answered Yes without looking at him or being sure what they were talking about although she did really know what he was telling her and then she got out of his car and watched him drive away.

TRADITIONAL STYLE INDIAN GARAGE

Chrystos

My old red car named PowWow Fever has a sunroof which leaks, which I've renamed a rain roof. There isn't a carport attached to my little green rental cabin, which has floors so crooked my cakes come out half-mast. My car is bigger than my kitchen, which gives you a sense of the proportionate meaning of things. Naturally, being a Menominee warrior, I'm too broke to get her roof fixed, because most of the money I make goes for repairs to keep her running, so I can get to work. This place, in common with many reservations, has no bus system. Actually, this is a genuine antique story at the moment (and my car only has two years to go in order to qualify), because she hasn't been running for five months. She's on sabbatical to write the novel about how much hell living with me is. Anyway, since we live in the Northwest, I can get a quart of cold rainwater splashed down the back of my neck when I start her up, unless I use my Traditional Style Indian Garage. This is very easy to replicate, if you are working on your Girl or Boy Scout merit badge in crafts. Scout around for a strong, extra-thick, large trash bag with no holes. Black is the preferred color, but many tribes have assimilated the dark green ones. Place this over the sunroof, making sure to go past all the seams. Weigh this down in the four corners with logs and bricks. If you'd like, you may sing a little song to the Beaver Nation. Beadwork is not recommended for ornamentation, but the logs and bricks can be painted with sun symbols using yellow ochre clay, dug up only from approved pits. This adds some extra magic, which keeps you dry. Relatively speaking. The author will be happy to travel any-where for green gas money and a red steak to demonstrate this method in person. Periodically check the bag and your soul for holes. This traditional garage can be stored in your trunk, an important consideration for us nomadic people. This garage has also been advertised on TV by a genuine Indian (not Latino) actor, so the historical significance cannot be overlooked. This has many outstanding features lacking in your ordinary garage. While arranging the bricks, I enjoy the stars and moon. I hear the sea lions hollering hello. Often my four cats assist by walking across it to test for air bubbles. If I'm really in luck, the transformer across the street will blow out in a blaze of glorious atomic aquamarine turquoise light. Somebody said the emanations of this event, which is the end of watching TV for a spell, cause cancer. Ema-nations is a mighty big word for a traditional Indian story, but I was accidentally caught in the crossfire of a few college English courses. So far, no one will give me disability for my wounds. I'm not too worried—I'm an Indian, so somebody is sure to kill me before I die an unnatural death. As for cancer, I have a list in my wallet of all my friends who have died from that, and not one of them lived near a transformer. I actually may already have cancer, but there's no way to tell without health insurance, which is why I keep thinking of migrating to Canada. Unfortunately, my people were a little too far south to claim dual borders. That is, below the lakes, not crazy. Although you could say we were crazy not to be more like the Dakota, so we could have had a car named after us. I've driven a Cherokee, but she wasn't a Jeep. I just have no respect! If you've been worried about paragraphs in this little monograph, there aren't going to be any. If you really need them, send along some money to this orphan with uncombed hair, so I can go back to college. Or, at least, buy a comb. The only possible problem with the garage is if the user forgets to remove the garage before driving away. This will cause dents in your hood or trunk and possible broken windows, so take precautions. This is the Voice of Experience. When removing your garage, stand well away, so you don't get wet. Always put the bricks or logs in your trunk first, to prevent ripping the garage. This garage is covered by Intellectual Property Rights, so a fee must be sent to the author — at least enough for a steak. If you are a vegetarian, send clean black cotton socks with no holes, which are a part of the traditional costume. For those of you without a car, this garage transforms miraculously, with a few snips, into an all-purpose rain-and-snow coat. In this case, some beadwork is allowed along the facial edge. This usage of the garage is particularly prevalent among the urban homeless tribes, who have also revived the new health trend for sleeping outside in all weather. We are conducting interviews to reveal the language-grouping from which the garage originated. Some Native scholars are of the opinion that this garage is a historical re-creation of an item found when Custer bit the mud. A government-funded convention is expected to decide the matter once and for all. Look for my free pH Skin dissertation on the Spider Web at Dot's commissary on bingo night. This is my gift to you in honor of our long and pleasant tea party here on Turtle Island. Accept no substitutes.

HOW TO SET A HOUSE ON FIRE

Stace Budzko

Before you light the gas, light a cigarette under the old red maple in the front yard, under a hunter's moon, and take a last look. Before this, walk through the ranch house with a miner's lamp and pesticide sprayer topped off with high-test racing fuel. Before it was your house it was your father's house and before it was your father's house it was his father's too. Before foreclosure on the family farm, before the new highway. Spray the gaps in the oak floorboards and get into the heating ducts, hit the horsehair plaster and take out electric sockets, then run a heavy gas line out to the barn. There is the combine. That is a backhoe. At one time chickens lived here. Before leaving, make sure the hay bales drip with fuel. This was feed once. On your way toss your house keys into the water well. Before doing anything else, make a wish.

After filling the birdbath next to the old red maple with the remaining octane, call Herm up at the fire station. After he gets on the line tell him to come over and bring a truck or two—with a crew. There's not much to see now, really. After he asks why, tell him. Tell him how the fire line went from where you stand to the well and then zigzagged to the barn, and after the farm equipment blew to the sky tell him how the furnace did the same. A chain of events, explain, it was a chain of events. After the windows kicked out there wasn't much anyone could have done. And after Herm asks if you would do it all over again, tell him you would. But come anyway, Herm. Tell him that.

THE JALAPEÑO CONTEST

Ray Gonzalez

Freddy and his brother Tesoro have not seen each other in five years, and they sit at the kitchen table in Freddy's house and have a jalapeño contest. A large bowl of big green and orange jalapeño peppers sits between the two brothers. A saltshaker and two small glasses of beer accompany this feast. When Tesoro nods his head, the two men begin to eat the raw jalapeños. The contest is to see which man can eat more peppers. It is a ritual from their father, but the two brothers tried it only once, years ago. Both quit after two peppers and laughed it off. This time, things are different. They are older and have to prove a point. Freddy eats his first one more slowly than Tesoro, who takes two bites to finish his and is now on his second. Neither says anything, though a close study of each man's face would tell you the sudden burst of jalapeño energy does not waste time in changing the eater's perception of reality. Freddy works on his second as Tesoro rips into his fourth. Freddy is already sweating from his head and is surprised to see that Tesoro's fat face has not changed its steady, consuming look. Tesoro's long, black hair is neatly combed, and not one bead of sweat has popped out. He is the first to sip from the beer before hitting his fifth jalapeño. Freddy leans back as the table begins to sway in his damp vision. He coughs, and a sharp pain rips through his chest. Tesoro attempts to laugh at his brother, but Freddy sees it is something else. As Freddy finishes his third jalapeño, Tesoro begins to breathe faster upon swallowing his sixth. The contest momentarily stops as both brothers shift in their seats and the sweat pours down their faces. Freddy clutches his stomach as he reaches for a fourth delight. Tesoro has not taken his seventh, and it is clear to Freddy that his brother is suffering big-time. There is a bright blue bird sitting on Tesoro's head, and Tesoro is struggling to laugh because Freddy has a huge red spider crawling on top of his head. Freddy wipes the sweat from his eyes and finishes his fourth pepper. Tesoro sips more beer, sprinkles salt on the tip of his jalapeño, and bites it down to the stem. Freddy, who has not touched his beer, stares in amazement as two Tesoros sit in front of him. They both rise hastily, their beer guts pushing the table against Freddy, who leans back as the two Tesoros waver in the kitchen light. Freddy hears a tremendous fart erupt from his brother, who sits down again. Freddy holds his fifth jalapeño and can't breathe. Tesoro's face is purple, but the blue bird has been replaced by a burning flame of light that weaves over Tesoro's shiny head. Freddy is convinced that he is having a heart attack as he watches his brother fight for breath. Freddy bites into his fifth as Tesoro flips his eighth jalapeño into his mouth, stem and all. This is it. Freddy goes into convulsions and drops to the floor as he tries to reach for his glass of beer. He shakes on the dirty floor as the huge animal that is Tesoro pitches forward and throws up millions of jalapeño seeds all over the table. The last thing Freddy sees before he passes out is his brother's body levitating above the table as an angel, dressed in green jalapeño robes, floats into the room, extends a hand to Tesoro, and floats away with him. When Freddy wakes minutes later, he gets up and makes it to the bathroom before his body lets go through his pants. As he reaches the bathroom door, he turns and gazes upon the jalapeño plants growing healthy and large on the kitchen table, thick peppers hanging under their leaves, their branches immersed in the largest pile of yellow jalapeño seeds Freddy has ever seen.

CURRENTS

Hannah Bottomy

Gary drank single malt in the night, out on the porch that leaned toward the ocean. His mother, distracted, had shut off the floodlights and he did not protest against the dark.

BEFORE THAT, his mother, Josey, tucked in her two shivering twelve-year-old grandaughters.

"I want you both to go swimming first thing tomorrow. Can't have two seals like you afraid of the water."

BEFORE THAT, one of the girls held the hand of a wordless Filipino boy. His was the first hand she'd ever held. They were watching the paramedics lift the boy's dead brother into an ambulance.

At this time, the other girl heaved over a toilet in the cabana.

*   *   *

BEFORE THAT, the girl who would feel nauseated watched as the drowned boy's hand slid off the stretcher and bounced along the porch rail. Nobody placed the hand back on the stretcher, and it bounced and dragged and bounced.

BEFORE THAT, Gary saw the brown hair sink and resurface as the body bobbed. At first he mistook it for seaweed.

BEFORE THAT, thirty-five people struggled out of the water at the Coast Guard's command. A lifeguard shouted over Jet Ski motors about the increasing strength of the riptide.

BEFORE THAT, the thirty-five people, including Gary and the two girls, formed a human chain and trolled the waters for the body of a Filipino boy. The boy had gone under twenty minutes earlier, and never come back up.

BEFORE THAT, a lifeguard sprinted up the beach, shouting for volunteers. The two girls, resting lightly on their sandy bodyboards, stood up to help.

BEFORE THAT, a Filipino boy pulled on the torpid lifeguard's ankle and gestured desperately at the waves. My brother, he said.

BEFORE THAT, it was a simple summer day.

1951

Richard Bausch

One catastrophe after another, her father said, meaning her. She knew she wasn't supposed to hear it. But she was alone in that big drafty church house, with just him and Iris, the maid. He was an Episcopal minister, a widower. Other women came in, one after another, all on approval, though no one ever said anything— Missy was seven, and he expected judgments from her about who he would settle on to be her mother. Terrifying. She lay in the dark at night, dreading the next visit, women looking her over, until she understood that they were nervous around her, and she saw what she could do. Something hardened inside her, and it was beautiful because it made the fear go away. Ladies with a smell of fake flowers about them came to the house. She threw fits, was horrid to them all.

One April evening, Iris was standing on the back stoop, smoking a cigarette. Missy looked at her through the screen door. "What you gawkin' at, girl?" Iris said. She laughed as if it wasn't much fun to laugh. She was dark as the spaces between the stars, and in the late light there was almost a blue cast to her brow and hair. "You know what kind of place you livin' in?"

"Yes."

Iris blew smoke. "You don't know *yet*." She smoked the cigarette and didn't talk for a time, staring at Missy. "Girl, if he settles on somebody, you gonna be sorry to see me go?"

Missy didn't answer. It was secret. People had a way of saying things to her that she thought she understood, but couldn't be sure of. She was quite precocious. Her mother had been dead since the day she was born. It was Missy's fault. She didn't remember that anyone had said this to her, but she knew it anyway, in her bones.

Iris smiled her white smile, but now Missy saw tears in her eyes. This fascinated her. It was the same feeling as knowing that her daddy was a minister, but walked back and forth sleepless in the sweltering nights. If your heart was peaceful, you didn't have trouble going to sleep. Iris had said something like that very thing to a friend of hers who stopped by on her way to the Baptist Church. Missy hid behind doors, listening. She did this kind of thing a lot. She watched everything, everyone. She saw when her father pushed Iris up against the wall near the front door and put his face on hers. She saw how disturbed they got, pushing against each other. And later she heard Iris talking to her Baptist friend. "He ain't always thinkin' about the Savior." The Baptist friend gasped, then whispered low and fast, sounding upset.

Now Iris tossed the cigarette and shook her head, the tears still running. Missy curtsied without meaning it. "Child," said Iris, "what you gonna grow up to be and do? You gonna be just like all the rest of them?"

"No," Missy said. She was not really sure who the rest of them were.

"Well, you'll miss me until you *forget* me," said Iris, wiping her eyes.

Missy pushed open the screen door and said, "Hugs." It was just to say it.

When Iris went away and swallowed poison and got taken to the hospital, Missy's father didn't sleep for five nights. Peeking from her bedroom door, with the chilly, guilty dark looming behind her, she saw him standing crooked under the hallway light, running his hands through his thick hair. His face was twisted; the shadows made him look like someone else. He was crying.

She didn't cry. And she did not feel afraid. She felt very gigantic and strong. She had caused everything.

BULLET

Kim Church

I know what a bullet can do. Everybody has an idea, everybody's seen close-ups—gaudy wounds, geysers of blood, arms and legs flopping, life kathumping to a close. TV bullet drama. But there are other, not-so-spectacular ways a bullet can work.

My husband wore a bullet on a chain around his neck. He had blond chest hair, red skin from the sun and drinking, and that bright silver necklace. Hobart. When he held me, his bullet would grind into the bone at the base of my throat. I still have a dark place there, I call it a birthmark but it's a bruise that never went away. "Am I your sweet meat?" he used to ask me. "Say it. Say, Hobart, you're my sweet meat."

Here's what I learned from marriage: I am not brave. I never will be. But I am patient, and I can outlast anyone.

A man came in the store last night. He didn't shop around, just marched straight up to the counter, shoved his hand in his pocket and said, "This bullet's for you," so I gave him all the money from my drawer, stuffed it in a sack like he said, and he—quick!—slapped the counter and left. Slapped down his bullet like he was paying cash, is what I told the police.

It was brass, not silver. Smaller than Hobart's and without the shine. Greasy, like some people's pocket change.

The robbery was all over this morning's news. They showed a picture of the store while the newswoman announced that the man who held it up hadn't used a gun. He didn't even say gun. The newswoman made a big point of this. She almost broke into a smile when she told how he'd disappeared before the police could find him. "Successful," she called him, making him sound heroic.

I wonder what I would say if she interviewed me.

"How did you feel when you realized what had happened?"

"I don't know. Sick. Mad. But mostly I was just glad he left without hurting me. Mostly I felt grateful."

"You were grateful?" Like it's the wrong answer. Like grateful isn't enough to satisfy a TV audience.

"Gratefulness can fool you," I would tell her. "It's a stronger feeling than you think. In fact, I'd put gratefulness up there with the big ones. It can feel like love, or grief, that strong."

I know this to be true. Or maybe how it works is, gratefulness makes you able to feel the big feelings you wouldn't be able to otherwise.

"Where's the bullet now?"

"The police took it. I've asked to have it back when they're through."

"Why? What'll you do with it?"

Keep it with the other one, I'm thinking. "Put it in my jewelry box, where I can look at it from time to time."

Because (not that I would say this on the news) I know what will happen. One day my robber will die. Maybe some gung-ho store clerk will shoot him when he reaches in his pocket. Maybe he'll come down with a fluke disease. Only forty-six years old, people will say. What a shame, what a waste.

Yes, I will say. I'll be tender, because I can afford to be. Yes, it is.

CONSUMING THE VIEW

Luigi Malerba

translated from the Italian by Lesley Riva

The sky was clear and the air clean, yet from the telescopes on the Gianicolo hill the Roman panorama appeared hazy and out of focus. The first protests came from a group of Swiss complaining that they had wasted their hundred lire on malfunctioning devices. The city sent out an expert technician, who had the lenses replaced: perhaps they were blurry from being exposed to the open air for so long. Nonetheless, protests kept coming, in writing and by phone. City Hall sent out another expert to test the telescopes again. A peculiar new element emerged: the panorama from the Gianicolo appeared blurry not only through the lenses of the telescopes, but also to the naked eye. The city claimed the problem was no longer its responsibility, yet the tourists kept complaining, in writing and by phone. After gazing for a while at the expanse of rooftops, with the domes of Roman churches surfacing here and there and the white monument of the Piazza Venezia, many went to have their eyes checked. Some even started wearing glasses.

A professor of panoramology was called in, from the University of Minnesota at Minneapolis. She leaned over the Gianicolo wall at varying hours: dawn, daybreak, noon, sunset, even at night. Finally she wrote a lengthy report on the distribution of hydrogen in the photosphere, on phenomena of refraction, on carbon dioxide polluting the atmosphere and even on the fragrance given off by exotic plants in the Botanical Garden below—without recommending any remedy.

A doorman at City Hall, who lived near the Gianicolo and who had learned of the problem, wrote a letter to the mayor explaining a theory of his. According to the doorman, the Roman panorama was being slowly worn away by the continuous gaze of tourists, and if no action was taken, it would soon be entirely used up. In a footnote at the end of his letter, the doorman added that the same thing was happening to Leonardo da Vinci's *Last Supper* and other famous paintings. In a second footnote he emphasized, as proof of his thesis, how the view visibly worsened in the spring and summer, coinciding with the greater crowds of tourists, while in the winter, when tourists were scant, one noticed no change for the worse; on the contrary, it seemed the panorama slowly regained its traditional limpidity.

Other expert panoramologists took photographs from the Gianicolo week after week, and these seemed to confirm the doorman's theory. The truth, however strange, now seemed crystal clear: the constant gaze of tourists was consuming the Roman panorama; a subtle leprosy was slowly corroding the image of the so-called Eternal City.

The City Hall public relations office launched a campaign,

which, in order to discourage tourists, tried to ridicule the panorama in general, the very concept of a view. Their press releases had titles like "Stay clear of the panorama" and "The banality of a view." Others, more aggressive, were entitled "Spitting on the panorama," "Enough of this panorama," "One cannot live on views alone." A famous semiologist wrote a long essay entitled "Panorama, catastrophe of a message." Some journalists abandoned themselves to malicious and gratuitous speculation on the greater corrosive power of Japanese or American or German tourists, according to their own whims or the antipathies of the newspapers where the articles were published. Fierce discussions were unleashed, which, though noisy, achieved the opposite of the desired effect: all the publicity, though negative, ended up increasing the number of tourists crowding the Gianicolo hill.

Eventually, the Roman city government, following the advice of an expert brought in from China, resorted to the stealthy planting of a row of young cypresses under the Gianicolo wall, so that, within a few years, the famous panorama would be completely hidden behind a thick, evergreen barrier.

THE GREAT OPEN MOUTH ANTI-SADNESS

Ron Carlson

After the wedding, drunk but not that drunk, Button lay arms-out across the bed. His tie dangled from one hand, and he wasn't surprised to feel it tugged at and then hauled suddenly away. The cat. He closed his hand. Yes, it was empty. He closed his eyes and opened his hand; then he closed his hand again and opened his eyes. Amazing the way a person is wired. He didn't need to look to know his hand was open. That tie was long gone. Button watched the ceiling fan and loved it for turning so slowly. Obviously in such slow motion it was intended only for his use for these few minutes. He worked one dress shoe off with the other, and then held it on a toe as long as he could. The air cooled his arch perfectly, and he thought that: perfect. Evaporation was such a stunning feature of life on earth. Water rises into the air. Now he opened his mouth and then a little wider than was comfortable. He tried to look, but he couldn't see. He knew his mouth was wide open. Button watched one blade of the fan take and lose a shadow as it rotated, and he wondered if opening your mouth helped you think. It seemed to be helping him. It was definitely helping him. His mind was clear. He decided to feed it a thought. His daughter was married. He'd witnessed the event this afternoon as Sharon left his arm and accepted a ring. Button decided to try another thought: she was now halfway across Dearden Bay on the way to the old Dearden Lodge. She'd be wearing her Michigan sweatshirt and jeans, and she and Larry would be leaning on the rail of the ferry's upper deck, bumping heads and talking about the lesser constellations far over Canada. Button opened his mouth a little wider; he was really thinking. And this mouth thing helped him from being sad. He wasn't sad. He was something, which was similar to sad, but his mouth and the fan and the cat and his hand and the tie, wherever it was, had helped him avoid the real sadness.

THINGS YOU
SHOULD KNOW

A. M. Homes

There are things I do not know. I was absent the day they passed out the information sheets. I was home in bed with a fever and an earache. I lay with the heating pad pressed to my head, burning my ear. I lay with the heating pad until my mother came in and said, "Don't keep it on high or you'll burn yourself." This was something I knew but chose to forget.

THE INFORMATION sheets had the words "Things You Should Know" typed across the top of the page. They were mimeographed pages, purple ink on white paper. The sheets were written by my fourth-grade teacher. They were written when she was young and thought about things. She thought of a language for these things and wrote them down in red Magic Marker.

By the time she was my teacher, she'd been teaching for a very long time but had never gotten past fourth grade. She hadn't done anything since her Things You Should Know sheets, which didn't really count, since she'd written them while she was still a student.

AFTER MY EAR GOT better, the infection cured, the red burn mark faded into a sort of a Florida tan, I went back to school. Right away I knew I'd missed something important. "Ask the other students to fill you in on what happened while you were ill," the principal said when I handed her the note from my mother. But none of the others would talk to me. Immediately I knew this was because they'd gotten the information sheets and we no longer spoke the same language.

I TRIED ASKING the teacher, "Is there anything I missed while I was out?" She handed me a stack of maps to color in and some math problems. "You should put a little Vaseline on your ear," she said. "It'll keep it from peeling."

"Is there anything else?" I asked. She shook her head.

I couldn't just come out and say it. I couldn't say, You know, those information sheets, the ones you passed out the other day while I was home burning my ear. Do you have an extra copy? I couldn't ask because I'd already asked everyone. I asked so many people—my parents, their friends, random strangers—that in the end they sent me to a psychiatrist.

"WHAT EXACTLY DO you think is written on this 'Things to Know' paper?" he asked me.

" 'Things You Should Know,' " I said. "It's not things to know, not things you will learn, but things you already should know but maybe are a little dumb, so you don't."

"Yes," he said, nodding. "And what are those things?"

"You're asking me?" I shouted. "I don't know. You're the one who should know. You tell me. I never saw the list."

TIME PASSED. I grew up. I grew older. I grew deaf in one ear. In the newspaper I read that the teacher had died. She was eighty-four. In time I began to notice there was less to know. All the same, I kept looking for the list. Once, in an old bookstore, I thought I found page four. It was old, faded, folded into quarters and stuffed into an early volume of Henry Miller's essays. The top part of the page had been torn off. It began with number six: "Do what you will because you will anyway." Number twenty-eight was: "If you begin and it is not the beginning, begin again." And so on. At the bottom of the page it said, "Chin San Fortune Company lines 1 through 32."

YEARS LATER, when I was even older, when those younger than me seemed to know less than I ever had, I wrote a story. And in a room full of people, full of people who knew the list and some who I was sure did not, I stood to read. "As a child, I burned my ear into a Florida tan."

"Stop," a man yelled, waving his hands at me.

"Why?"

"Don't you know?" he said. I shook my head. He was a man who knew the list, who probably had his own personal copy. He had based his life on it, on trying to explain it to others.

He spoke, he drew diagrams, splintering poles of chalk as he put pictures on a blackboard. He tried to tell of the things he knew. He tried to talk but did not have the language of the teacher.

I breathed deeply and thought of Chin San number twenty-eight. "If you begin and it is not the beginning, begin again."

"I will begin again," I announced. Because I had stated this and had not asked for a second chance, because I was standing and he was seated, because it was still early in the evening, the man who had stopped me nodded, all right.

"Things You Should Know," I said.

"Good title, good title," the man said. "Go on, go on."

"There is a list," I said, nearing the end. "It is a list you make yourself. And at the top of the page you write, 'Things You Should Know.' "

ROSE

John Biguenet

"It must have been, I think she said, two years after the kidnapping, when your wife first came by." The voice on the phone sounded young. "What was that, '83, '84?"

"Kidnapping?"

"Yeah, she told me all about it, how it was for the private detective you hired after the police gave up."

"You mean the picture?"

"Right, the age progression."

"You could do it back then?"

"It was a pain in the ass. You had to write your own code. But, yeah, once we had the algorithms for stuff like teeth displacement of the lips, cartilage development in the nose and ears, stuff like that, all you had to do was add fat-to-tissue ratios by age, and you wound up with a fairly decent picture of what the face probably looked like. I mean, after you tried a couple different haircuts and cleaned up the image—the printers were a joke in those days."

"And you kept updating Kevin's . . ." He hesitated as he tried to remember the term. "Kevin's age progression?"

"Every year, like clockwork, on October twentieth. Of course, the new ones, it's no comparison. On-screen, we're 3-D now; the whole head can rotate. And if you've got a tape of the kid talking or singing, there's even a program to age the voice and sync it with the lips. You sort of teach it to talk, and then it can say anything you want, the head."

The voice was waiting for him to say something.

"I mean, we thought it was cool, Mr. Grierson, the way you two didn't lose hope you'd find your boy one day. Even after all these years."

He hung up while the man was still talking. On the kitchen table, the photo album Emily had used to bind the pictures, the age progressions, lay open to one that had the logo and phone number of Crescent CompuGraphics printed along its border. His son looked fifteen, maybe sixteen, in the picture.

He had found the red album the night before, after his wife's funeral. Indulging his grief after the desolate service and the miserly reception of chips and soft drinks at her sister's, he had sunk to his knees before Emily's hope chest at the foot of their bed, fingering the silk negligee bruised brown with age, inhaling the distant scent of gardenias on the bodice of an old evening gown, burying his arms in all the tenderly folded velvet and satin. It was his burrowing hand that discovered the album at the bottom of the trunk.

At first, he did not know who it was, the face growing younger and younger with each page. But soon enough, he began to suspect. And then, on the very last leaf of the red binder, he recognized the combed hair and fragile smile of the little boy who returned his gaze from a school photograph.

As he thought of Emily secretly thumbing through the age progressions, each year on Kevin's birthday adding a new portrait on top of the one from the year before, he felt the nausea rising in his throat and took a deep breath. It's just another kind of memory, he told himself, defending her.

He, for example, still could not forget the green clock on the kitchen wall that had first reminded him his son should be home from school already. Nor could he forget the pitiless clack of the dead bolt as he had unlocked the door to see if the boy was dawdling down the sidewalk. And he would always remember stepping onto the front porch and catching, just at the periphery of his vision, the first glimpse of the pulsing red light, like a flower bobbing in and out of shadow.

In fact, turning his head in that small moment of uncertainty, he took the light to be just that: a red rose tantalized by the afternoon's late sun but already hatched with the low shadows of the molting elms that lined the street. And he remembered that as he turned toward the flashing light, lifting his eyes over the roses trellised along the fence—the hybrid Blue Girl that would not survive the season, twined among the thick canes and velvet blossoms of the Don Juan—and even as he started down the wooden steps toward the front gate, slowly, deliberately, as if the people running toward the house, shouting his name, had nothing to do with him, he continued to think rose, rose, rose.

TIFFANY

Stacey Richter

"**D**ivide or die," chanted the ring of evil siblings crushed against her, "divide or die." But she didn't want to divide. She wanted to remain intact, singular, in her little spot of ocean warmed by the hot object. Fish were floating dead or swimming wrong on the surface. She actually brushed one on the eye. It was luscious, the heat that welled up in her when she flicked that dead eye. For a moment she ached to divide, she fervently yearned to be two, but it passed. Everything passes, she told herself, trying to block out the chants of the others. "Divide or die," they elaborated.

The whole thing had begun with a pang of loneliness, a desolation the weakest couldn't survive. They cried themselves to death. But the stronger ones looked for others like themselves.

Then, as a group, they checked the perimeter for food. If it was warm and the wind was low, and if some rich, thick sludge was being heated and pumped into the slow current, they could all divide at once. It was an orgy with thousands of participants, hundreds of thousands, millions. Shivers of pleasure shot across their surface.

Now they spread across the ocean surface endlessly—a solid red mass that rolled and rippled in the wind like a sheet on a line. They soaked up the energy of the hot object and snacked with relish on the dead things they made. When the shadow of a cloud moved across their surface, they knew they were being caressed by another entity just like themselves—large, swift, devouring.

She was a mutant. The hot object had worked its way into her DNA and unhooked something. So what if she was a mutant? So what if she didn't like to divide? She wanted to float in the warm current, and to flop on her back now and then and watch the clouds lumbering across the pretty blue sky. How long did any of them have? Just a few days. Why not just fucking enjoy it?

But the group was powerful. Shared emotions swept over them like storms: hunger, awe, desire. For a moment at dawn they were all racked with nostalgia. There were times when every single one of them felt out of place. Peer pressure was a force to be reckoned with.

"Look at her," said a pert little dinoflagellate with a perfectly smooth protein coat. "Look at her with her nose up in the air, refusing to divide."

They laughed at her. No one was on her side. It was hard to have only siblings and no parents to act as referees. If she didn't divide, she couldn't truly be part of the All, and if she wasn't part of the All, she couldn't share in the divinity that was being passed from sibling to sibling like a joint. "Divide or die," they said. That they would stop saying it was unthinkable.

It was tempting, so tempting, to just dissolve into it, but she'd begun to believe it didn't really mean anything anyway. She'd begun to believe there wasn't any difference between being many and being singular. In the end, she just was, and she was going to dissolve soon anyway into a little drop of liquid neurotoxin. But before she did, she wanted to give herself a beautiful name.

THE FALLGUY'S FAITH

Robert Coover

Falling from favor, or grace, some high artifice, down he dropped like a discredited predicate through what he called space (sometimes he called it time) and with an earsplitting crack splattered the base earth with his vital attributes. Oh, I've had a great fall, he thought as he lay there, numb with terror, trying desperately to pull himself together again. This time (or space) I've really done it! He had fallen before of course: short of expectations, into bad habits, out with his friends, upon evil days, foul of the law, in and out of love, down in the dumps—indeed, as though egged on by some malevolent metaphor generated by his own condition, he had *always* been falling, had he not?—but this was the most terrible fall of all. It was like the very fall of pride, of stars, of Babylon, of cradles and curtains and angels and rain, like the dread fall of

silence, of sparrows, like the fall of doom. It was, in a word, as he
knew now, surrendering to the verb of all flesh, the last fall (*his* last
anyway: as for the chips, he sighed, releasing them, let them fall
where they may)—yet why was it, he wanted to know, why was it
that everything that had happened to him had seemed to have
happened in language? Even this! Almost as though, without
words for it, it might not have happened at all! Had he been nothing more, after all was said and done, than a paraphrastic curiosity, an idle trope, within some vast syntactical flaw of existence?
Had he fallen, he worried as he closed his eyes for the last time and
consigned his name to history (may it take it or leave it), his juices
to the soil (was it soil?), *merely to have it said he had fallen*? Ah!
tears tumbled down his cheeks, damply echoing thereby the
greater fall, now so ancient that he himself was beginning to forget
it (a farther fall perhaps than all the rest, this forgetting: a fall as it
were within a fall), and it came to him in these fading moments
that it could even be said that, born to fall, he had perhaps fallen
simply to be born (birth being less than it was cracked up to be, to
coin a phrase)! Yes, yes, it could be said, what can *not* be said, but
he didn't quite believe it, didn't quite believe either that accidence
held the world together. No, if he had faith in one thing, this fall-
guy (he came back to this now), it was this: in the beginning was
the *gesture*, and that gesture was: he opened his mouth to say it
aloud (to prove some point or other?), but too late—his face
cracked into a crooked smile and the words died on his lips . . .

THE CATS IN THE PRISON RECREATION HALL

Lydia Davis

The problem was the cats in the prison recreation hall. There were feces everywhere. The feces of a cat try to hide in a corner and when discovered look angry and ashamed like a monkey.

The cats stayed in the prison recreation hall when it rained, and since it rained often, the hall smelled bad and the prisoners grumbled. The smell did not come from the feces—but from the animals themselves. It was a strong smell, a dizzying smell.

The cats could not be driven away. When shooed, they did not flee out the door but scattered in all directions, running low, their bellies hanging. Many went upward, leaping from beam to beam and resting somewhere high above, so that the prisoners playing ping-pong were aware that although the dome was silent, it was not empty.

The cats could not be driven away because they entered and left the hall through holes that could not be discovered. Their steps were silent; they could wait for a person longer than a person would wait for them.

A person has other concerns, but at each moment in its life, a cat has only one concern. This is what gives it such perfect balance, and this is why the spectacle of a confused or frightened cat upsets us: we feel both pity and the desire to laugh. It faces the source of danger or confusion and its only recourse is to spit a foul breath out between its mottled gums.

The prisoners were all small men that year. They had committed crimes which could not be taken very seriously and they were treated with leniency. Now, although small men are often inclined to take pride in their good health, these prisoners began to develop rashes and eczemas. The backs of their knees and the insides of their elbows stung and their skin flaked all over. They wrote angry letters to the governor of their state, who also happened to be a small man that year. The cats, they said, were causing reactions.

The governor took pity on the prisoners and asked the warden to take care of the problem.

The warden had not been inside the hall in years. He entered it and wandered around, sickened by the curious smell.

In the dead end of a corridor, he cornered an ugly tomcat. The warden was carrying a stick and the cat was armed only with its teeth and claws, besides its angry face. The warden and the cat dodged back and forth for a time, the warden struck out at the cat, and the cat streaked around him and away, making no false moves.

Now the warden saw cats everywhere.

After the evening activities, when the prisoners had been shut up in their cell blocks, the warden returned carrying a rifle. All night long, that night, the prisoners heard the sound of shots coming from the hall. The shots were muted and seemed to come from a great distance, as though from across the river. The warden was a good shot and killed many cats—cats rained down on him from the dome, cats flipped over and over in the hallways—and yet he still saw shadows flitting by the basement windows as he left the building.

There was a difference now, however. The prisoners' skin condition cleared. Though the bad smell still hung about the building, it was not warm and fresh as it had been. A few cats still lived there, but they had been disoriented by the odors of gunpowder and blood and by the sudden disappearance of their mates and kittens. They stopped breeding and skulked in corners, hissing even when no one was anywhere near them, attacking without provocation any moving thing.

These cats did not eat well and did not clean themselves carefully, and one by one, each in its own way and in its own time died, leaving behind it a different strong smell which hung in the air for a week or two and then dissipated. After some months, there were no cats left in the prison recreation hall. By then, the small prisoners had been succeeded by larger prisoners, and the warden had been replaced by another, more ambitious; only the governor remained in office.

LEVEL

Keith Scribner

Dreaming that her belly was an Elephant Heart plum and that chokecherries were embedded in her lower back, Madeline woke from a nap. She opened the bedroom door to find her husband not at his desk as she'd hoped but kneeling before the battered cabinet that stored bills and records. Across the top of the cabinet, which Madeline had painted purple and gray, a level stretched so long it projected off the sides. Although Madeline hadn't spoken, Dion said as if in response, "It's just a level. Something we've needed." He said it without looking up. With a hammer he tapped wedges of wood under the cabinet's feet.

She leaned into the doorframe and smoothed her hands over her pregnant belly. Beside her, propped in the corner between the bedroom and bathroom doors, stood a white plastic tube as tall as she was with a price tag of one hundred ten dollars.

Dion steadied the level across the top of the peg board where they hung their coats. He shook his head, then he ripped the peg board, coats and all, from the plaster.

With her thumbs she massaged the bitter green seeds of pain in her lower back. "A hundred and ten dollars?" she said.

"Relax, Peaches. You're not supposed to stress. Have you done your breathing?"

Money was tight with the baby coming, and only a week ago Dion had made a stink when Madeline bought a forty-dollar outfit for her sister-in-law's baby shower, and finally Madeline had to say: Sweetie, I make the cash at the moment, and I want to buy her a gift. It was a Giants baseball uniform, size 6 to 12 months, cap included. "That's an expensive level," she said.

"You cannot have a baby in all this sloping and slanting. He'll never get his bearings." Dion was eyeing the level on top of the telephone table, tapping the wedges of wood under the base. "This is a life investment. Mahogany and brass. Professional grade. There's no accuracy in a dinky twelve-inch aluminum level."

She lowered herself to the toilet seat and held her belly as she peed. The floor slanted toward the tub, charmingly, she thought. Like a nest. Cupping toward the middle of the cottage.

"It's all cockeyed," he called from the living room. "No wonder I haven't been able to get to work. I can't set a pen on my desk without it rolling away." She heard him tapping wedges. "And I was worried about the baby. I swear, a cup of coffee could've slid right off the desk."

Would it ever work?—Dion taking care of the baby during the day after Madeline's brief maternity leave was up, writing his botany thesis by night. He'd need time at the university too, charting his experiments on drupaceous fruits—peaches, cherries, plums.

She flushed the toilet, and he called, "Living room's ready."

When it was late, she read a novel in bed propped up with extra pillows, her back still aching. Dion kneeled on the mattress beside her, naked, eyeing the level on the headboard. He hopped down to the floor, and as he tapped, Madeline felt their bed rise slightly under her left shoulder, and the hard bitter ache in her lower back softened, sweetened.

"That's more like it," he said and lay down beside her with the level, smoothing his hand over the dark polished wood. "Isn't this something," he said. "Such an elegant instrument."

She touched the inlaid brass and the tiny round windows. One end of the level rested on the fruit of her belly. The other end was balanced on Dion's knees. He raised his end imperceptibly until the bubble in the tube of glass eased through the green syrupy liquid and settled between the two black lines.

BLIND FISH

Melanie Rae Thon

My father says nobody whose word can be trusted has pulled a sturgeon from this lake since 1927, but divers searching for drowned children and drowned mothers swear they've seen fish bigger than themselves hiding in the lake's deepest trenches.

A freshwater sturgeon can grow twelve feet long. One old fish with barbels that look like whiskers might live a hundred years if no hungry human hooks or spears her.

They resist change.

Their Jurassic ancestors would find them sweetly familiar, still recognizable, though there are a hundred fifty million years between them.

They resemble sharks, or mermaids, or monsters.

Their snouts are flat, their skulls bony. Swim bladders in their guts allow them to breathe air for several hours. Long enough to roll in the shallows and spawn over rocks. Long enough to flop on the beach while they wait for the fisherman with a club to kill them. In courtship, they tumble and leap near the bottom. Or so we are told. What human has ever seen this?

They are loved for their delicate flesh and even more loved for their delicate caviar. You can kill the female and eat all of her, or you can catch her to strip the eggs, and this is said to be more merciful.

They are bottom feeders but not scavengers. This distinction is important. With their barbels they search the sediment for living prey: insect larvae, snails, worms, crayfish.

They are not vicious.

Big as they are, they won't attack you.

Hours after it is caught, a half-frozen, fifteen-inch pike can bite hard enough to draw blood as you try to gut it. But a sturgeon will look at you with its sad eyes as if to say, *I'm older than your grandmother. What are you doing?*

They are not blind after all; they see you. When they surface to feed in the shoals, their vision miraculously returns to them. Amazed, they understand that loss of sense is a choice of environment, a fact in the lake's treacherous canyons, but not, in the end, irreversible. Seeing you, they are not grateful for sight. They think, *We did not miss much.*

Don't be deceived by the scales. A sturgeon is soft inside, and delicious.

Some claim there are monsters in this lake. They have pictures to prove it. But the pictures are always grainy, out of focus, so the monster might be a log tossed by a wave, a trick of light, a sturgeon breaching.

The monster might be your own memory, wild horses, your mother who can breathe air but who doesn't want to, who goes down instead, who seeks the deepest trench, the one unmeasured, carved by the glacier that dug this lake, then melted to fill it.

If you fall in the water, you're safe where it's white. That's the foam, near the surface. Where it's green, you have hope. Swim toward the light. Keep your faith. Imagine all the people on shore who still love you. If it's black and you're blind, you can lose your direction, make mistakes or grow weary. That far down, the weight of water is oppressive, which is why, I suppose, the sturgeon's scales are hard as enamel, why its body is flat and has five bony ridges, why it rises out of the lake to swim miles upstream where it spawns in the dangerous river.

THE VOICES IN MY HEAD

Jack Handey

I never know when the voices in my head are going to start talking to me. I might be coming out of my apartment and I'll look up at the clouds. Suddenly, the voices in my head will tell me to go back inside and get an umbrella, because it might rain. Sometimes I'll obey the voices and go get the umbrella. But sometimes I muster my strength and refuse to get the umbrella. Still, the voices don't let you forget that you disobeyed them, especially if it rains. They'll say, "I knew you should have gotten the umbrella. Why didn't you?"

I don't expect you to understand what it's like to have voices in your head telling you what to do. But it is a nightmare I live with all the time. Right now, for instance, the voices are telling me to go back and change the word "nightmare" to "living hell."

The voices torment me from the time I wake up. They'll say, "Get up and go to the bathroom to urinate." Throughout the day, they never let up: "Go get something to eat," "Go take a nap," "Go to the bathroom again," "Get ready for bed." On and on. Sometimes the voices even talk to me in my sleep, telling me to get up and urinate. My fear is that the voices will tell me to do something crazy, like go look for a job.

I used to think that drinking alcohol would calm the voices, but it usually makes them worse. They'll say things like "Go tell that person what you really think of him" or "Get up on that table and do your funny cowboy dance."

The voices used to talk to me about the Beatles. When I was young, they'd tell me to go buy a certain Beatles album. "But I don't have any money," I'd say. Then the voices would suggest I mow some lawns to earn some money. "But that's a lot of work," I'd say. "Well," the voices would say, "do you want the album or not?" (Wait. That might have been my father.)

Sometimes I go for relatively long periods without the voices talking to me, such as when I'm watching TV, or watching ants, or lying on the floor and trying to blow lint balls into one big herd of lint. Or seeing which one of my cats is most afraid of "pillowcase head." But these golden moments are fleeting, and soon the voices return.

I just wish the voices would tell me something useful once in a while, like how to say things in French or where my gloves went. But they hardly ever do. In fact, many times the voices like to taunt me, telling me, for instance, to turn left at an intersection when, it turns out later, I clearly should have turned right. Or telling me to wear a tie that obviously looks ridiculous.

Even worse, sometimes the voices themselves don't know what they want. They'll tell me to go up and talk to a pretty woman, then they'll say, "No, wait, she's too pretty for you," then they'll say,

"Oh, go ahead," then they'll say, "What if your wife finds out?" (Man, make up your mind!)

When you tell people you have voices in your head, they think you're crazy. But when you don't say anything at all, and you just sit there and stare at them, they also think you're crazy. So you can't win.

I thought about going to a psychiatrist to get rid of the voices, but the voices said it would be expensive, and would probably take a long time, and that I'd have to put my pants on and go to the subway, then come all the way back on the subway, then take my pants off, and who knows if it would even work? Sometimes the voices have a point.

One day, I decided that I couldn't take it anymore, and I decided to silence the voices in my head once and for all. But I couldn't figure out how to do that, so I never did.

Maybe the answer is not to try to get rid of the voices but to learn to live with them. (I don't really think that; I'm just saying it for the voices.)

Will I ever be able to fully control the voices in my head? Probably not. But will I at least be able to adjust my life style so that the voices are not a threat to me or others? Again, the answer is no.

But I'm not ready to throw in the towel just yet, because one thing I have learned is this: the voices may be bossy, but they're really stupid.

THE OLD TRUTH IN COSTA RICA

Lon Otto

I will tell you a true story. One time a *perezoso*, what you call a sloth, was caught on the forest floor. He had come down from the treetops to do his weekly business and was in the process of burying it when a jaguar came along and took advantage of the situation and ate him.

When the other *perezosos* learned of this calamity, alas all too common, they came together to speak well of the dead one and to see if anything could be done about the danger, which each of them faced once a week, the elders somewhat less frequently. Half awake, one of the mourners felt a tear swelling out of his eye and moved to brush it away, though by the time his claw reached his face, the tear had long since fallen. So he delicately scratched his nose and said to the others, "Perhaps we should abandon this practice that brings so many of us to grief."

After considering the suggestion for some time, another *perezoso* said, "But if we do not descend to the forest floor to do our business where we can bury it, our enemy the jaguar will smell it and know we are here."

The others pondered this and at length agreed that it was so, remembering that that was the explanation for the custom. But the one who had spoken first observed, "Our neighbors the monkeys let fly from the highest treetop, and they seem none the worse for it. If the jaguar cannot reach us, what does it matter that he knows we are here?"

"We are not monkeys," the second speaker declared, and all of them, even he who had spoken first, slowly nodded their heads.

"We have always followed this practice," a third said. "To do otherwise would not be typical of us."

The second one agreed, saying again, "We are not monkeys."

It was approaching night, the conversation having taken up the better part of a day. Out of the fragile light a fourth *perezoso* spoke, the oldest and wisest of them, who had to descend to the forest floor on business no more than once every two or three weeks, but then required many hours to accomplish what was necessary. He said, "The truth is this. Dropped casually from the safety of our beloved branches, our shit would be merely shit. Hard and shapely as our patient nature makes it, it is still shit. But when we plant it in the ground where the jaguar walks, it becomes precious as jewels."

Dark fell. Somebody asked, "Why? Why does it?"

But he got no answer. Hours later, when all of them had drifted from half awake to half asleep, the old one spoke again, so softly nobody understood him; it sounded more like a snore. He said, "It just does. It just does."

WHY YOU SHOULDN'T HAVE GONE IN THE FIRST PLACE

Samantha Schoech

Do not drive to Vallejo to meet him halfway. Even if your life feels airless and you haven't been laid since you called it off with him two months ago. First of all, you've had two glasses of red wine and it probably isn't a good idea to drive on a freeway that will be crowded even on a Sunday night. Second, although Vallejo sounds funny and adventurous at first, campy even, when you arrive at Rod's Hickory Pit, fuzzy with anticipation and misgiving, it will be a sleazy, depressing place, made no less so by your impending tryst. Asian gang members will be playing pool in the bar and the two other women in there, one with hot pants on, will be taking turns singing old Madonna songs on the karaoke stage. It will be the kind of thing you would laugh about under different circumstances.

Because you will arrive first, you will spend at least ten minutes worrying that he is not going to show up. And even though he will eventually show up, the fact that you have had to entertain the thought of being humiliatingly stood up will lodge in your consciousness next to the vows you made in college about sisterhood and not sleeping with men already in relationships.

You will stand outside smoking, scanning the parking lot and watching the headlights whisk by on Highway 80. When you ask one of the Asian gang members for a light he will say, "I was wondering when you were going to talk to me." You will pretend not to hear him and drift over to the far side of the cement landing between the parking lot and the lobby entrance. Through the restaurant window you will watch a family move slowly through the buffet. They will be the only people eating and the sight of them will make you feel lonely. You will smoke furiously, which will do nothing for your pounding heart.

When he gets there, he will be driving her white sedan and you'll let your mind land on that fact for an uncomfortable second before you smile and wait for him to meet you on the landing. As soon as you see him, you will realize that the whole thing was a mistake. He'll want to go back into the bar for a beer and you'll go and do all the talking while he grins anxiously at you and squeezes your knee and says nothing. The whole time you will tell yourself silently that you are over him, that you only met him up here at this ridiculous place as a lark. Just two friends having a late-night adventure. That's what you'll call it: an adventure. The two of you will smirk at the euphemism.

After only half a beer, you will begin to feel flirty, take his hand and, against your better judgment, suggest a room at the Motel 6. Before he agrees, hesitation will flash on his face briefly, but long enough for it to register. Both of you will know for the rest of the night that the motel room was your idea. Even when he pays for it, you will feel a bit like a huntress, which is the opposite of feeling wanted, and contrary to the whole point of dating a married man.

Don't drive to Vallejo because after all the anticipation the sex will be mediocre and he will suffer a very unattractive anxiety attack about becoming the kind of man he has already become. You'll lie there in the stale smoke and disinfectant smell, listening to the mysterious clunkings of the upstairs guests, wondering why in the hell you are there. And when he asks if it would bother you terribly if he went home that night, it is, after all, so much easier to sleep in his own bed, you will say yes, it does bother you. And so he will stay, but reluctantly, and the whole night, listening to the motel pool filter and the sound of him not sleeping, will only remind you of why you shouldn't have gone in the first place.

MYTHOLOGIES

R. L. Futrell

They are heading east on 35, crossing over the Kanawha and into West Virginia when they see that the traffic has slowed. The man is flipping through the AM stations, listening to bits of sports talk radio, weather reports, and the like. As an act of kindness he has the volume low. The woman is reading.

The man says, *For a class?*

Mythology, the woman says.

She is not really reading. Just skimming. Looking out the window at the traffic, at the town, noticing that the water is up, that there are barges pushing coal at what seems too slow a pace to be going anywhere.

The man says, *Which ones?*

The Five Ages of Man and the Flood. Prometheus. All of them, really.

This is months before the separation, years before what will become "a bitter time in all their lives." Before the accident at the house. Before the job transfer. This is the melancholy they will look back on with some fondness—driving now through the fertile bottomland of early marriage, of new love.

They take the ramp off 35 and circle down into Henderson, just across the river from Point Pleasant—the radio popping and fizzing with static as they pass under the bridge. On the left, the river pushes slowly into West Virginia. The man has his window down and can smell the river, he thinks, mixed with diesel exhaust from the tractor trailers ahead of them. Can smell late summer and fresh-cut lawns. Occasionally he catches a glimpse of shirtless men on barges between the clapboard houses and mobile homes that line the river.

The man says, *Is it interesting?*

The reading? Not really, the woman says.

The traffic is as thick and heavy as the slow-moving river. She is looking out her window now, further up the mountain to where they are building the new interstate. There are orange signs at regular intervals warning of two-way radio communication and blasting zones. A number of rocks have rolled down from the construction site and have smashed small trees and flower beds, have spilled onto the road in places. There are larger boulders lodged against the corners of homes, embedded in screened-in porches and resting against rusted swing sets. She sighs loudly as they pass a blue Ford Taurus with the hood crumpled completely by a bright tan boulder nearly twice as big as the car itself.

Jesus, the woman says. *Those poor people. Just so we can get there sooner.*

The man says, *I wonder where this river goes.*

She rolls her window down to feel the humid warmth of summer on her skin.

The ocean, the woman says, still looking at the flattened Taurus. *Always to the ocean.*

REVIVING PATER

John Goulet

"Miss, we'd like one shaped like a kidney."

It was the end of October and Dolly and the gang and I had arrived at the Pillow Outlet in a holiday mood. Dutifully, the blue-uniformed clerk, on her wheeled ladder, glided left and right across the wall of pillow bins in search of Pater's kidney—we call him Pater, sometimes Pater the Pianist, for he was once a professional musician. "How about this one?" she called down from the rafters, shaking her find.

Dolly peered. "Too big," she said. Dolly, having sewn Pater's gauze body sack, knew his proportions by heart.

Another pillow was proffered from on high.

"We've already got temporal lobes," I pointed out.

"We've got everything save the right kidney," Dolly informed.

This was true: Pater, mostly stuffed, waiting in the backseat of the parked Volvo, needed only this kidney to rise from the dead, so to speak.

"Of course," the clerk apologized. They knew us well here. Once a week, we dropped by to purchase pillows—arm pillows, foot pillows, tiny eyeball pillows—gradually reconstituting Pater. Every family has—or should have—certain rituals around whose warmth it is possible to gather during this late October holiday.

Fortunately a perfect kidney pillow was soon located, and we steamed north to Pater's chapel in the woods. To Dolly fell the delicate task of velcroing the kidney in place. I drove, watching in the rearview mirror as Dolly worked on slumped and still-lifeless Pater, the gang hovering. From a passing car a family of jack-o'-lanterns waved. When Pater's kidney was finally snugged in place, the abdominal cavity secured, Dolly blew on Pater's beady eyes.

"He blinked," she proudly announced.

The Volvo grew rowdy with rejoicing, our way of expressing ourselves and also covering the bestial sounds that Pater, stretching himself, always made when coming back to life. In the mirror, I saw his color grow rosy.

A half dozen turns brought us to the tiny chapel in the woods, where we found the piano in front of the altar, exactly where it had been last October. The gang lit a hundred candles, while Pater, with Dolly's help, shuffled to the keyboard. It was no mean feat to play Beethoven's "Moonlight Sonata" with pillowfingers, but Pater had always been a skillful technician. Huddled in the front pews, we wept. A family of bats circled in the dank, cold air above our heads, cruised the candle flames. "Better than ever," Dolly said.

I never knew what to say at a moment like this.

Pater always grew nervous as he reached the end. Who could blame him? When the last note had died away, Dolly and I watched the gang, wiping away tears, march up. "Time to liberate the pillows, Gramps," they said. They were not mean children. Certainly Pater struggled, he always did, clinging to the piano for dear life. Dragged away, he clutched at the piano stool, using that as a shield. Finally it was necessary to pin him down, one on each limb. No Boy Scout knife was needed; Dolly's gauzy body sack surrendered itself to fingernails and teeth. Released, the many pillows, with a wheezy exhalation, tumbled onto the floor of the chapel. "See you next year, Grandpa!" one said. "Arrivederci," said another. "Sayonara."

In the woods behind the chapel we dispersed the pillows in all directions. The wind took the shredded body sack and blew it high into a black tree.

On the way home we discussed next year's Pater. Some wanted him bigger, others smaller. Others suggested a different outlet. "Do you think he feels any pain?" Dolly wondered. The youngest asked, "Where does he go on the other days of the year?" Of course, this discussion period was also part of our tradition; it was by considering such issues in a sensible way that we grew closer as a family.

BULLHEAD

Leigh Allison Wilson

Every story is true and a lie. My mother tells a story about the love of her life. It's a simple one, but she always cries when she tells it and looks right through me, as though I hadn't been born. Something about the detail makes me feel there's a sadness in the world that will last until the rushing crack of doom.

It goes like this: In the forties, when she was a teenaged girl in Tennessee, my mother fell in love with the boy next door. That same year the government decided to build dams all over the state. As if some crazy rainstorm had come and gone, pristine new lakes puddled the landscape from Knoxville to Memphis. One lake formed right over my mother's hometown—people lost their homes, lost their businesses, their graveyards, their farmland and, in some cases, their hearts. On the night before the government moved everybody out of her hometown my mother and the love of her life, this boy next door, made love in my mother's bedroom. Her parents were at a prayer meeting, praying for dry land, I guess, like Noah. This boy was sweet, was kind, was smart and generous and lovely to look at; this boy was the love of her life. He moved with his family to Texas the next day and she never saw him again.

Except: Once a year she rents a rowboat and goes out on the lake that has drowned her old hometown. She drops a penny over the side, right over the place where her old house must be. Fifty years, fifty pennies. She imagines them drifting downward, all those pennies, drifting through the murky lake water, startling the catfish and bullhead, each penny listing into the open window of her bedroom and falling at last onto the pillow where she once lay with her head against the love of her life, the boy next door. She imagines their ghost love showered by pennies; she imagines this love beyond all loves glittering with gold. Then she rows back to shore and back to my father and me and the life that can't compete with memory.

Every story is true and a lie. The true part of this one is: Love and the memory of love can't be drowned. The lie part is that this is a good thing.

ACCIDENT

Dave Eggers

You all get out of your cars. You are alone in yours, and there are three teenagers in theirs, an older Camaro in new condition. The accident was your fault, and you walk over to tell them this.

Walking over to their car, which you have ruined, it occurs to you that if the three teenagers are angry teenagers, this encounter could be very unpleasant. You pulled into an intersection, obstructing them, and their car hit yours. They have every right to be upset, or livid, or even violence-contemplating.

As you approach, you see that their driver's side door won't open. The driver pushes against it, and you are reminded of scenes where drivers are stuck in submerged cars. Soon they all exit through the passenger side door and walk around the Camaro, inspecting the damage. None of them is hurt, but the car is wrecked. "Just bought this today," the driver says. He is 18, blond, average in all ways. "Today?" you ask.

You are a bad person, you think. You also think: what a dorky car for a teenager to buy in 2005. "Yeah, today," he says, then sighs. You tell him that you are sorry. That you are so, so sorry. That it was your fault and that you will cover all costs.

You exchange insurance information, and you find yourself, minute by minute, ever more thankful that none of these teenagers has punched you, or even made a remark about your being drunk, which you are not, or being stupid, which you are, often. You become more friendly with all of them, and you realize that you are much more connected to them, particularly to the driver, than possible in perhaps any other way.

You have done him and his friends harm, in a way, and you jeopardized their health, and now you are so close you feel like you share a heart. He knows your name and you know his, and you almost killed him and, because you got so close to doing so but didn't, you want to fall on him, weeping, because you are so lonely, so lonely always, and all contact is contact, and all contact makes us so grateful we want to cry and dance and cry and cry.

In a moment of clarity, you finally understand why boxers, who want so badly to hurt each other, can rest their heads on the shoulders of their opponents, can lean against one another like tired lovers, so thankful for a moment of peace.

ALL GIRL BAND

Utahna Faith

My all girl band is in trouble. Not musical trouble, not financial trouble, not boy trouble, not even the trouble of looking like beautiful vampires every night and every day. We have simply done something wrong. We do not know what it is, and I am sure we did not mean to do it. Nevertheless, we are in trouble.

My father looks at me nervously. How can I be so white-skinned, ebony-haired, red-lipped and ethereal, when my mother, at my age with the same face and body, was suntanned, golden-haired, peach-lipped and earthbound? I believe I make him nervous. Yes, I make him nervous, and it's about time.

I am back in our old house, bad house, in my old room, changing clothes. What does one wear to jail? I am frightened.

The other three "Four Whores of the Apocalypse" arrive and

we console one another. As we walk through the family room past the loud football game, my father looks at us without moving his mouth or turning his head. As I say good-bye he nods once, chin down, hold a beat, chin level. That is all.

We climb into the red Ford Fairlane, slide our own CD into the player and sing. I know through the terror in my stomach that we have never been so on, so hot, so perfect.

Of course we are right to turn ourselves in.

I NEVER LOOKED

Donald Hall

They stayed at the old wooden hotel because it was quiet except for the throb of the waves. There were few other guests. "I feel stranded," he said as they unpacked the first day, "*happily* stranded." Afternoons, they sat in a pink wooden glider on their balcony and had a drink as she smoked Winstons. For three mornings they slept late, showered, made love, and ate *huevos rancheros* at a café down the coast beside the crashing of the same sea.

Their last day, he finished his eggs and lifted his head to watch her handsome profile as she looked out to sea. The smallest wrinkles started beside her eyes. Her mouth flicked in a way he recognized. "You must be thinking about sex," he said.

"What?" She reddened slightly under her tan.

He laughed. "I guess it wasn't *me*," he said.

He saw her pause, wondering whether to lie.

"I was thinking about a day in Sausalito."

"Gino?" he said.

She looked away and laughed.

They sat in silence drinking strong coffee, holding hands when they set down their cups. She wore white shorts, and he admired her long, smooth, tanned legs beside his hairy pale ones; even her toes were slim and pretty.

In front of their hotel, they walked by the sea's edge and kissed as the scrappy waves curled at their ankles. They spread towels on the sand and she took off her top. Slowly, slowly, they rubbed sunscreen into each other's skin. They lay silently under the heat, twenty minutes a side. When the wind rose, salt water flecked their skin. Then they sat wearing dark glasses in the shade of a green beach umbrella.

They washed sand off their bodies and drove half an hour east for lunch in the hills at a roadside place that made the best *chile rellenos*. They looked through the open window at the long expanse of sand and sea. On the coastal highway below, they saw a semi sprawled in a ditch, its aluminum shining. Around it were tow trucks, police cars, and an ambulance. Tiny men carried a body into the ambulance.

As she drove them back, she said, "When do we leave?"

He shrugged. "It's only two hours. Did I tell you what my cousin said to the bartender?"

"Two and a half. Yes, you told me, about the Smirnoff's. I remember."

He started to tell the story again, then pulled back and interrupted himself. "I don't want to go," he said.

"We never want to go," she said, "because we know we have to go."

"It's like . . ." He stopped.

106

In their room he made a small pitcher of martinis, finishing the half bottle of Gordon's. He packed the Noilly Prat with the laundry in his suitcase. He set the pitcher and two glasses on a table before them as they sat on their balcony in their glider with its pink paint flaking. She smoked two cigarettes. Overlooking the beach, they concentrated on the waves that rolled continually, a big wave followed by three little ones, a big wave followed by three little ones. They sipped the martinis as the glasses and pitcher sweated. When they emptied their glasses, he did not pour the rest. "Diluted," he said.

She brought two bottles of Evian from the small, noisy refrigerator.

"Three little waves," he said, "then a big one." He sipped at the water and made a face. "Not after gin," he said.

"They must get tired, doing the same thing over and over again."

"Oceans never get tired of anything."

"I do."

She looked straight ahead at the ocean as she drank her Evian. An old red tomcat slid from the balcony of the room next to theirs and rubbed at her foot, which she lifted away. He remembered another cat, years ago, spilling from the lap of a small woman with red hair who laughed and said, *"Now* things will change!"

"Can we go back to bed?" he said.

"Let's. Then we'll finish packing and check out."

He nodded, standing. "We'll be early."

They undressed separately and made love again. He followed the rhythms of the waves, a long thrust and three quick ones.

When they finished she smoked a cigarette. "Number three," she said. "Down to five today. Do you know the joke?" she said. "Two women talking? One says, 'Do you smoke after intercourse?' and the other says, 'I don't know. I never looked.'"

He laughed, but he had nodded when she started to tell it.

Driving, they were silent. Twice she cracked the window to smoke a Winston. When they entered the city with its traffic, she smoked another. He let her out a block from her house, flicking his trunk lid open. They pecked each other's lips, and she walked off with her backpack and duffel. An SUV pounded past him, down the empty street. In the rearview mirror he watched an old dog approach, sniffing her duffel, his lank tail wagging.

MY DATE WITH NEANDERTHAL WOMAN

David Galef

I didn't know whether to bring flowers, which don't say much to someone from a basic subsistence culture. But a raw beef-steak might come across as too suggestive, and I'd read somewhere that Neanderthals were supposed to be vegetarians. I opted for the middle road, a box of chocolates.

I arrived just as the sun was sinking below the tree line. Glena lived in a cave by the edge of the forest and had, I'd heard, a more natural sense of time than those of us dominated by Rolexes and cell phones. Still, she wasn't there when I hurt my hand knocking on the cave entrance.

I tried twice, the second time with my foot. Then I called out, emphasizing the glottal G I'd heard when her name was pro-nounced by the TransWorld Dating Agency. She appeared as if suddenly planted in front of me, barrel-chested and bandy-legged, not much taller than a high-cut tree stump. Her furry brown hair was matted with sweat, but she smiled in a flat-faced way as I held out the chocolate.

Grabbing the box, she ripped it open and crowed in delight. She stuffed several candies with their wrappers into her mouth and chewed vigorously. The agency had told me not to waste time with complicated verbal behavior, so I just pointed at her and myself and said, "Glena, Robert."

She nodded, then pointed to the chocolate and rubbed her belly. Such a primal response! Frankly, I'd grown tired of modern women and their endless language games. She offered me one of the remaining chocolates from the box, and I was touched: pure reciprocity, though she looked disappointed that I didn't eat the wrappers. I mimed eating and pointed away from the forest. I would take her out to dinner.

Neanderthals, I recalled, were often on the cusp of starvation. She seemed to understand and followed me obediently as I led her to Chez Asperge, a small French-fusion-vegan restaurant not far from the woods.

Chez Asperge is elegant but casual, and we were greeted heartily by Claude the *maitre d'*. I didn't know the place had a dress code. In fact, the little loincloth Glena wore made me feel overdressed. Anyway, the situation was fixed with a borrowed jacket, which Glena wore in a charmingly asymmetric fashion.

God, I hate all the introductory explanations of a first date— which is why I was so happy none of that mattered to Glena. With a familiarity as if she'd known me for years, she spread her arms on the table and scooped up the mashed lentil dip. It's true, a woman who enjoys her food is sexy. Of course, she offered me some, and I showed her how to spread it on pita. But knives seemed to frighten her, and I'm sorry about that scar on the table. Still, we had a lovely meal—she particularly enjoyed the raw vegetable plate.

After dinner, I walked her home along the forest path. Movies and clubs could come later. I didn't want to overstimulate her. Even electric lights made her twitch. But along the path the moon was out, illuminating Glena's short but powerful body in a way that was weirdly beautiful. When I reached for her hand, she jerked back—different cultures have different intimacy rites, the agency guy said—so I took pains to explain that my intentions were honorable. Maybe she couldn't understand the words, yet I think she got the gist. Anyway, there's a limit to what I can achieve by gestures.

Eventually, her hand crept into mine and nearly crushed it. My miming of pain, hopping on one foot and flailing, made her laugh. A sense of humor is important in a relationship.

We paused at the entrance to her cave. She smiled, the gaps in her teeth drawing me in. Her earthy aroma was a definite aphrodisiac. What came next was sort of a kiss, followed by a rib-cracking embrace that the osteopath says is healing nicely. Still, whenever I think about it, I feel twinges. What a woman! I'd like to invite her out this weekend, but I can't e-mail her. Maybe I'll just drop by her cave accidentally on purpose with a bouquet of broccoli.

Yes, I know all the objections. Some couples are separated by decades, but we're separated by millennia. I like rock music and she likes the music of rocks. I'm modern Homo Sapiens and she's Neanderthal, but I think we can work out our differences if we try.

FAB 4

Jenny Hall

We'll read in the newspaper a few decades from now that crime was at an all-time low tonight. All of it: property crimes, homicide, probably even unreported infractions of the domestic sort. For these few hours, peace reigned. Goodwill toward men and all that. I guess the idea is that even the criminals were watching. Later, we will be suitably alarmed by anthropological studies that point to a series of uncanny substitutions—public for private, superhighways for squares, pixels for people—and so we will try to compensate by inventing chips and blocks and parental warning labels. But not yet.

Ed Sullivan says: Ladies and Gentlemen, tonight we have a rilly big shew!

My sister Katie says: I simply cannot stand it. I *cannot* stand it. Her folded hands are tucked under her chin and her arms cover her chest, as if she's protecting herself from something, from something invisible but lethal, like radiation—or heartbreak.

We *will* be alarmed by those studies, studies that draw arrows from TV sets to other more abstract qualities that we didn't bargain for. But not yet. Tonight the flickering that illuminates our faces does not yet bring us a sense of dread, of estrangement and alienation. There is no sense of ineffable disappointment associated with an evening like this. We are containers, empty vessels, but it is still possible to be sated. Enough is something we understand, because there are, after all, only three channels.

Ed Sullivan says: These four lads from Liverpool are causing quite a stir!

Katie says: Don't you think Katie McCartney sounds good? Don't you think that Ringo's nose makes him especially lovable? Don't you think? Don't you?

We see, Katie and I, our reflections in the window when we turn to look, since it is already dark outside. The living room is reflected, too: matching gold sofa and love seat, grandfather clock, our mother's doll collection displayed in a cabinet on the wall opposite the window, four rows of miniature perfection. Our little sister, Lisa, who is supposed to be in bed, is sitting at the top of the stairs. We have the TV on louder than usual so that she can hear. We are washed in a calm gray-blue: twilight inside.

Katie says: Look, look, look at our reflections in the window, look!

She laughs, jumps up and does the twist, in her pink pajamas, so that she can watch her reflection do the same.

The room is reflected in the TV screen, too, because there is a glare from the floor lamp next to the sofa. This is the light we must leave on, because to do otherwise—to sit idly in the dark—is bad for the eyes, and possibly also for the soul. And so this combination of light and reflective surfaces means there are three versions of us in this space: two copies—one in the window and one in the TV screen—and one original. It is still possible to distinguish between them with ease. We are not yet casual about this technology that still gleams, and so it has not demanded from us any sacrificial appeasement. There have been no Faustian bargains.

During the first commercial, we look *through* the room's reflection, out the window, across the street, at the Jameson house. As I float across the street in my mind, I can see the Jameson boys, studying their television set with an earnestness they would otherwise take pains to disguise. I imagine that, like us, their reflections float above their actual bodies, hovering somewhere between the pure window and the television, lurking, biding time. There are three Jameson boys, and they provide a symmetrical foil of sorts to us girls as our bodies move through time and space in this place that is the intersection of adolescence and suburbia and the 1960s. Katie has a crush on Paul (Jameson, but also McCartney), one that will be consummated, a few years from now, in room 102 of the Howard Johnson on Highway 8. Nothing will come of the union, not even a broken heart. Tonight, though, she gazes across the street every few minutes because she is hopeful.

Ed Sullivan claps. Katie claps. The Beatles bow.

We are poised at the brink of something, all of us: these four clever British boys with the funny hair, the Jameson boys, across the street, Katie, me—even little Lisa. We are careening toward a gorgeous future, insulated and comforted by the blue flickering which provides, if nothing else, clear evidence that *we are not alone. Tele* means: at or from a distance. *Vision* means: sight. If we could see the distant future, we would wonder what went wrong. But tonight we are at the Ed Sullivan Theater in New York City, and we are in Liverpool, and we are across the street flirting with the Jameson boys. All this simultaneously. Television. And we can't see the future. And this is a marvelous thing.

THE PETERSON FIRE

Barry Gifford

It was snowing the night the Peterson house burned down. Bud Peterson was seventeen then, two years older than me. Bud got out alive because his room was on the ground floor in the rear of the house. His two sisters and their parents slept upstairs, above the living room, which was where the fire started. An ember jumped from the fireplace and ignited the carpet. Bud's parents and his ten- and twelve-year-old sisters could not get down the staircase. When they tried to go back up, they were trapped and burned alive. There was nothing Bud Peterson could have done to save any of them. He was lucky, a fireman said, to have survived by crawling out his bedroom window.

I didn't see the house until the next afternoon. Snow flurries mixed with the ashes. Most of the structure was gone, only part of the first floor remained, and the chimney. I was surprised to see Bud Peterson standing in the street with his pals, staring at the ruins. Bud was a tall, thin boy, with almost colorless hair. He wore a Navy pea coat but no hat. Black ash was swirling around and some of it had fallen on his head. Nobody was saying much. There were about twenty of us, kids from the neighborhood, standing on the sidewalk or in the street, looking at what was left of the Peterson house.

I had walked over by myself after school to see it. Big Frank had told me about the fire in Cap's that morning when we were buying Bismarcks. Frank's brother, Otto, was a fireman. Frank said Otto had awakened him at five-thirty and asked if Frank knew Bud Peterson. Frank told him he did and Otto said, "His house burned down last night. Everybody but him is dead."

I heard somebody laugh. A couple of Bud's friends were whispering to each other and trying not to laugh but one of them couldn't help himself. I looked at Peterson but he didn't seem to mind. I remembered that he was a little goofy, maybe not too bright, but a good guy. He always seemed like one of those kids who just went along with the gang, who never really stood out. A bigger kid I didn't know came up to Bud and patted him on the left shoulder, then said something I couldn't hear. Peterson smiled a little and nodded his head. Snow started to come down harder. I put up the hood of my coat. We all just kept looking at the burned-down house.

A black and white drove up and we moved aside. It stopped and a cop got out and said a few words to Bud Peterson. Bud got into the back seat of the squad car with the cop and the car drove away. The sky was getting dark pretty fast and the crowd broke up.

One of Bud's sisters, Irma, the one who was twelve, had a dog, a brown and black mutt. I couldn't remember its name. Nobody had said anything about Irma's dog, if it got out alive or not. I used to see her walking that dog when I was coming home from base-ball or football practice.

Bud Peterson went to live with a relative. Once in a while, in the first few weeks after the fire, I would see him back in the neighborhood, hanging out with the guys, then I didn't see him anymore. Somebody said he'd moved away from Chicago.

One morning, more than thirty years later, I was sitting at a bar in Paris drinking a coffee when, for no particular reason, I thought about standing in front of the Peterson house that afternoon and wondering: If it had been snowing hard enough the night before, could the snow have put out the fire? Then I remembered the name of Irma Peterson's dog.

WORDS

John A. McCaffrey

It is in her apartment, with her gone for pizza, that he finds himself alone and prying, looking around and admiring her tastes, her choices in furniture, her abilities as a decorator. It is a geometric apartment, all angles and edges. She is an accountant, and the home speaks of economy and order. But it is also soft, the colors warm, dark, with bits of highlights. Like her, he decides. He likes her things, her leather couch, television, computer. He feels comfortable in the space.

On an end table, near the couch, he sees a spiral notebook. He flips it open. It is filled with words. English words. His native tongue, not hers. The script is military precise yet dainty, light, the ends of letters punctuated with upturned curls. Next to the English word is its Chinese equivalent, and then, in English again, the definition. He scans the words, pages of them, and begins to see a pattern. The words, at the end of the notebook, the most recent entries, were spoken by him.

The first one is "possessive." It is almost scratched into the paper. There is no curl at the end of the "e." He mouths the definition: A *desire for ownership, occupancy, hold.* The word "hold" is underlined. He traces it with his finger and flushes. He remembers the conversation. Just days earlier, on the phone. She had questioned his whereabouts over the weekend. Doubted the veracity of his claim that he was with friends, accused him of infidelity. "Some young girl," she had spat out, her accent thick. He said she was crazy, that she was being very possessive. He remembers the silence on the phone. Thinks: Was she jotting down the word?

After "possessive" is "resolve." The word is stretched on the page, the "o" oblong, the "v" wide and flat. She has written out two definitions. The first: *to break up into separate elements or parts.* The second is written all in caps. It says: *TO MAKE A DECISION ABOUT, TO MAKE CLEAR.* He winces. He has been using the word constantly with her, always in reference to his pending divorce. Justifying why he has not pushed it through faster, why he still talks to his wife, "the woman," as she describes her, "who left you."

"I'm just trying to resolve things," he had said, over and over to her, "I need to resolve some issues before I move on."

His head starts to tighten. He flips a page, sees the last word entered: "content." It is written so faint he has to hold the page up to his eyes to make out the definition: *Happy enough with what one has or is; not desiring something more or different.* He smiles, thinks of the night before. They had gone to a movie and then back to her apartment. They had slowly undressed each other, played, danced and wrestled their way to the bedroom. Then, on her low-lying bed, they kissed. And he was flooded with joy; it ripped through him. He had gripped her bare shoulders, licked at her skin, off-white and flawless, gripped tighter and tighter, absorbed her body. Later, as they lay sated, he looked at her and said: "I feel so content."

HE CLOSES THE NOTEBOOK and walks to the lone window in the apartment's living room. He looks out and across at another building, sees people behind curtains, near sinks, in bedrooms, getting dressed, watching television, talking. He hears the door of the apartment crack open. She walks in, pizza box in hand. She sets it on a table and removes her coat. She smiles and looks at him. He walks toward her, searching for the right word.

THE BLACK CITY

Leonardo Alishan

for Farhad Shakerin

I cut my lower lip shaving and I was by the gates of the Black City, a city made of black marble, a black city made of marble in the middle of the desert, the closest mine of marble hundreds of miles away. Strange city. Strange marble city far away from any oasis. Black City my soul called home.

I entered through the gates fully aware that it was my city, mine so intimately that I felt I had planned it, that I had been the city planner as well as every building's architect. I was the marble and the mine. I was the slave who mined the marble and the slave who pulled it through the desert. I was the king of the Black City and its sole visitor. My strange city.

I walked through streets heavy with intimate scents—the scent of my mother's hair, my father's shirt, oranges we shared on a

Friday evening, and of hot summer nights filled with Granny's fairy tales. I walked through streets populated with familiar faces — faces I knew from different phases of my life, almost all in white or black. No one seemed to be in a hurry; no one seemed to be going anywhere; yet all were moving. No one spoke. Silent, scented streets, populated with people who were still alive in the other world, who grew older in the other world, but were all as I had seen them as child, as youth, as man.

Black marble city bordered on one end by a mosque, on its dome a round moon resting; at the other end, a cathedral, the winter sun sitting on its steeple. A street sweeper I recognized from our old neighborhood swept fallen stars like dead leaves, while the arms of the tower clock did not stand still for a moment but moved clockwise and counterclockwise with the rhythm of medieval dancers. This was a black marble city I had built with every passing moment of my life and was still building, if I was still alive; and I was alive though still connected with an umbilical cord to the wet womb of a dead god.

Amidst the black and white crowd I saw a little girl in dazzling colors, dancing and hopping with laughter and joy; and I was delighted to see one so happy in my city, my life. I walked up to her and asked who she was. She said she was the childhood of my wife. "Have you always been so happy?" I asked. "I was happy," she said, "but with each passing moment I grow happier." "Do I have anything to do with your joy?" I asked. "Yes, you do," she said, "every day that she spends with you is spent in sorrow for the day and in despair for tomorrow; thus, I, her yesterday, grow happier and more radiant in her memory. How wrong you are, on the other side, to think the past cannot be changed." I cried; quietly I cried and turned my face.

I traveled my marble city, my black strange city, with tired feet and pain. Near the mosque, by the other gate, I saw a little boy selling black flowers, a little boy with wrinkles and scars on his face, selling black flowers which I craved. I asked, "How much?" He answered, "They're yours; they've been waiting for a long time." "Who are you?" I asked. "I am your childhood," he said. "But you were so happy; I remember you clearly," I said, "you were so happy." "But now we know better, don't we?" he said. I took the black flowers and dragged myself to the gate.

"I am not king here," I cried out. "No, you're not," said the priest who had baptized and married me, "we have a queen here," and he pointed to a procession of Persian soldiers with whom I had served in the army. They were carrying a golden box carriage on their shoulders. "Where are they going?" I asked. "They are taking the queen of the Black City to our temple," said the priest, "where she is sacrificed every April." The procession stopped. The queen drew the silk curtains aside. "Hello darling," she said with a sad smile. "Hello Granny," I whispered. The procession moved on, mumbling a familiar prayer in Armenian.

Before stepping out of the gate, I turned for one last look at the boy. He stood there looking at me like an orphan I was leaving behind. "Look what I've done to you," I muttered through my tears. He wiped his eyes with the back of his little hand and said, "Look what they've done to us." I stepped out of the black gate and heard it slam shut behind me. The razor fell. In the mirror, there was an old man, his chin and throat covered with blood.

JUSTICE—A BEGINNING

Grace Paley

One day, waiting for a bus, standing on a street corner in Lower Manhattan, somewhere near Canal; having completed jury duty, having in fact judged another human being and found him guilty, she thought of justice, that heavy word. As a member of the general worldwide mothers' union, she had watched the man's mother. She leaned on the witness bar, her face like a dying flower in its late-season, lank leafage of yellow hair, turning one way then the other in the breeze and blast of justice. Like a sunflower maybe in mid-autumn, having given up on the sun, Faith thought, letting wind and weather move her heavy head.

Still the man had held a real gun to the head of the old grocer and taken his half-day's profit of about twenty-seven dollars. Immediately Faith thought as she often did of the great gun held at the world's head and the cheaper guns pointing every which way at all the little nations that had barely gotten their heads up. She probably said Oh shit or even Fuck. Many people, some friends, really hated the way she moved from daily fact to planetary metaphor. Others thought she was absolutely right.

She leaned against someone's car, looked up and around, and saw the high six-story wall of a building whose old companion had been torn down, leaving a pale green New York imprint of old staircases, landings, some mysterious verticals and horizontals. She sighed not cosmically this time, but with an appreciation for the delicate but extraordinary designs of time and decadence. A man, passing, stopped, watched her looking and sighing. Well, he said, what do you think, lady? It's like the rest of us. It's going to deteriorate any minute, right?

At home she was surprised by Anthony visiting. It was the middle of the workweek. Here's Judy, he said. Remember her? Of course, she said. Then she told him that she was exhausted and thought she might deteriorate any minute, probably because of justice and her own wintry visage.

But Ma, he said, your visage isn't wintrier than it was last week. Right, said Judy. It's more late October or early November, don't you think, Anthony? He smiled to encourage her. She was shy but sometimes made good sentences. Anthony rolled his eyes round and round. When they rested, he said, Honest, folks, that wasn't a comment, it was only yoga.

Okay, okay, Faith said, there's some good stuff in the fridge. She wanted to go to her room and sit on the nice chair she'd recently bought for herself so as to be comfortable when writing things down. She needed to think more about the jury system, mainly her companion jurors. Also the way that capitalism was getting to be a pain in the world's neck. She thought she might try to make a poem out of that opposition.

After about an hour Anthony knocked on the door. Ma, when you're finished being private, come out and have some tea with us. We have some really bad news for you. This wasn't true, but if he'd said, Let's have tea and pie, and we have some wonderful news for you, she'd never leave her room.

Okay, she said, coming to the door. I'm ready, I guess. For God's sake, tell me.

THAT COULD HAVE BEEN YOU

Jim Heynen

The boys knew that on the farm danger was everywhere, sometimes in the teeth of a spinning gear, other times in the jaws of a growling boar. Danger could plunge from the sky in jagged-edged hailstones or collapse beneath them in weak timbers over a well. Hay balers didn't care what they baled, and silage choppers didn't care what they chopped. But mostly the danger the boys knew was in stories about what happened somewhere, someplace, just out of sight, in the next county, down the road six miles, some-where else. The bull that crushed a man against a gate. The woman who drowned trying to save her child from rushing spring floods. The man who broke his neck falling from the haymow.

The tornado that killed a whole family except the two-month-old baby who was found in a lilac bush without a scratch on her.

The boys listened to the stories, and they didn't argue with the truth of them. They'd had their own fair share of close calls. There was the eighty-pound hay bale that fell thirty feet and exploded in a green spray around them, and the lightning that splintered a huge box elder tree right after they decided to run out from under that very tree and play in the rain. Once a steel splinter from the corn sheller flywheel whirred like a table saw past their heads. And they had their cuts and bruises. Knuckles that looked as if they'd been gnawed on by meat grinders. Sprained ankles and wrists. Blood blisters that took toenails and fingernails off as they healed. Small concussions that were good for week-long headaches. Wood slivers of all sizes that had punctured every part of their bodies. And that's not even counting all the skinned knees and nosebleeds. The boys had plenty of bangings-around, but nothing so bad that they weren't able to talk about it, maybe even boast about it, the next week.

In town on Saturday nights, the grown-ups would point out what terrible things had happened to other people:

See those farmers with all those missing fingers? Cornpickers did that.

See that boy who doesn't have an arm in his sleeve? Power take-off did that.

The evidence was everywhere: missing thises and missing thats. Hobblers and limpers and a scar-face or two. Farms tore lots of people up, no doubt about it.

Then the grown-ups would always come up with the clincher: That could have been you, they'd say. That could have been you.

Of course, it could have been them. The boys knew that. They also knew that it was impossible to explain that they still lived without fear, lived as if every day held the promise of adventures in the sunlight, even if the sky was dark, even if the icicles hanging from the eaves on the barns could drop at any moment like dazzling swords and impale them to the snow—the way one did to this twelve-year-old not so far away, just far enough away that the boys didn't know his name.

THE WALLET

Andrew McCuaig

When Elaine arrived at work the first thing she noticed was that Troy had left his wallet on the small shelf next to a half-finished cup of Coke. Troy left his food regularly, as if she were his maid, but he left his wallet less often—about once a month. The first time it happened was just her second night on the job, and she thought maybe he was testing her honesty, or, worse, that he had created some excuse to come back and see her. He had, in fact, returned half an hour later and deliberately rubbed his body up against hers as he retrieved his wallet instead of just standing at the door and asking her to hand it to him. They had made awkward small talk in the cramped booth before he finally raised his wallet in a salute, said good-bye and good luck and rubbed past her again.

Now, as she settled onto the stool for her shift, she could smell his lingering presence. Sloe picked up the cup of Coke and placed it in the garbage can at her feet, careful to keep it upright. The cup had sweated out a puddle in the summer heat and she shook her head despairingly. She lined up her piles of quarters and dimes on the shelf in order to have something to do. Two booths down, José waved at her and gave her two thumbs up, a gesture he thought was cute. He was another lecherous type, always spending his breaks standing at her door looking her up and down and blowing smoke into her booth. She waved at him so he'd turn around.

In front of her now the highway was black. Every few minutes headlights would appear in the distance like slow trains but most of the time the drivers would pick the automatic lanes. Then three or four cars might come in a row and she'd be grateful to move into a rhythm—reach, grab, turn, gather, turn, reach, good night. It was annoying when people didn't bring their cars close enough, but at least it allowed her to stretch more. By midnight she had made change for twenty-six people. Several weeks ago she had started to keep track out of boredom. Her midnight record was seventy-two, her fewest, twelve.

At about three o'clock a car came toward her too fast, weaving like a firefly, before picking her booth. The brakes screeched, the muffler roared: it was a little yellow Chevette, an eighties car pocked with rust. Elaine leaned forward with her hand ready, but the driver, a young woman, made no move to pay her toll. She looked straight ahead, her face hidden by strings of brown hair, both hands locked tight to the wheel. Beside her in the front seat was a small beat-up suitcase overflowing with clothes.

Elaine said, "Good morning," and the woman said, " I need money."

Elaine hesitated. "You mean you don't have the toll?"

"No, I mean I need money." She turned now and Elaine saw her bleary eyes and splotched face. There was an ugly gash below one eye and the skin around it had swollen up and turned purple. There seemed to be an older scar on her nose, and dried blood in the corner of her mouth. Her stare was bitter and bold and it made Elaine look away.

She was about to raise the bar and tell her to go on ahead when she saw movement in the backseat. Looking closer, she saw there were two children, one about five, the other barely two, neither in car seats or seatbelts. Their eyes were wide and afraid and Elaine realized it was this that had drawn her attention to them in the dark. The little one held on to a gray stuffed animal, the older one was sucking her thumb.

José was watching her; he raised his palms and scowled. She had been trained to signal in a certain way if she was being held up, and José seemed to be waiting for this gesture. Instead, she gave him a thumbs up and surreptitiously reached for Troy's wallet. She opened the wallet to find ninety-two dollars inside. She pulled these bills out, wadded them in her fist and reached out to the woman, who took the money, gripped the wheel harder and sped away. The older girl's face, framed by the back window, receded into the darkness, her eyes like glowing stones.

HOW TO END UP

Jennifer A. Howard

First, graduate from college. You are now a grown-up.

Then, promise someone you will love him forever. Say, No one but you will ever kiss these lips (brush your fingers against them for emphasis). Snake your hand down the front of your jeans and say, This is yours too. Pick a side of the bed to be yours, but share your deodorant, share your password. Read long novels out loud on road trips. Agree upon your song. When you are no longer covered by your parents' health insurance, decide to celebrate your promise in public. Choose a pastor from the Yellow Pages; if possible, find one who makes rubber stamps on the side. Serve meatballs.

Buy a major appliance together. Go all out and buy a house. Change your name; tell your most feminist friends that this is a matriarchal tradition in your family. File jointly. Surf the Pottery Barn website for wall color inspiration.

Rinse and repeat for a matter of years. How many is up to you. But then, start to nap when you are in the passenger seat on long drives. Tire of how much he enjoys the Weather Channel. Tell yourself you never really liked sex anyway.

When you are ready, begin to look forward to the nighttime, after he is asleep. Fall in love with the gentle sentences you read in the books you have started taking to bed. Drink too much at a party and kiss somebody scandalously young. Remember kissing. Engineer kisses. Decide you are an ethical slut. Pretend to convince your husband he could be too, but hope he disagrees. This might be too much work.

Move on slowly. Spread the classifieds out on the dining room table, possible apartments circled in red. Wonder who will get the half-empty hand soap pump in the bathroom; feel confident the Grape-Nuts will be yours. Hide your favorite books at work. Revert to the first person singular in public. Call your mother and ask her for boxes.

Once you have broken his heart, make believe it was necessary for your survival. Become reckless with the hearts of others and fickle with your own. Learn to live without most of your furniture, but hang on to your cigarettes. They will come in handy when burning bridges. Black out half the names in your address book in permanent marker. Practice not wearing your ring on short walks to the store.

Most important, flank yourself with women, both cynics and dreamers. Go to them and snooze away poppied afternoons of warmth and good feelings. Admit the things you need. Rest assured they will love you even though they understand that sometimes you are just a girl trying to wish her way away. The road home, they will remind you, is not always the way you came.

THE ORANGE

Benjamin Rosenbaum

An orange ruled the world.

It was an unexpected thing, the temporary abdication of Heavenly Providence, entrusting the whole matter to a simple orange.

The orange, in a grove in Florida, humbly accepted the honor. The other oranges, the birds, and the men in their tractors wept with joy; the tractors' motors rumbled hymns of praise.

Airplane pilots passing over would circle the grove and tell their passengers, "Below us is the grove where the orange who rules the world grows on a simple branch." And the passengers would be silent with awe.

The governor of Florida declared every day a holiday. On summer afternoons the Dalai Lama would come to the grove and sit with the orange, and talk about life.

When the time came for the orange to be picked, none of the migrant workers would do it: they went on strike. The foremen wept. The other oranges swore they would turn sour. But the orange who ruled the world said, "No, my friends; it is time."

Finally a man from Chicago, with a heart as windy and cold as Lake Michigan in wintertime, was brought in. He put down his briefcase, climbed up on a ladder, and picked the orange. The birds were silent and the clouds had gone away. The orange thanked the man from Chicago.

They say that when the orange went through the national produce processing and distribution system, certain machines turned to gold, truck drivers had epiphanies, aging rural store managers called their estranged lesbian daughters on Wall Street and all was forgiven.

I bought the orange who ruled the world for 39 cents at Safeway three days ago, and for three days he sat in my fruit basket and was my teacher. Today, he told me, "It is time," and I ate him.

Now we are on our own again.

21

Jim Crace

A youngish man, a trifle overweight, too anxious for his age, completed his circuit of the supermarket shelves and cabinets and stood in line, ashamed as usual.

He arranged his purchases on the checkout belt and waited, with his eyes fixed on the street beyond the shop window, while the woman at the till scanned all the bar codes on his medicines, his vitamins, his air freshener, his toilet tissue, his frozen Meals for One, his tins, his magazines, his beer, and his deodorant, his bread, bananas, milk, his fat-free yogurt, his jar of decaf, and his treats: today, some roasted chicken legs, some grapes, a block of chocolate, and two croissants. He rubbed his thumb along the embossed numbers of his credit card while each item triggered a trill of recognition from the till.

The till's computer recognized the young man's Distinctive Shopping Fingerprint as well, the usual ratio of fat to starch, the familiar selection of canned food, the recent and increasing range of health supplements, the unique combination of monthly magazines. The pattern of the shopping identified the customer. Even before the woman at the till had swiped the credit card, the computer had lined up the young man's details—his list of purchases for the previous seven months, his credit rating, his Customer Loyalty score. It knew broadly who he was and how he lived. It could deduce what his modest rooms above the travel shop were like, how stale they were, how flowerless, how functional, how crying out for change. Here was the man whose cat had died or run away three months ago. No cat food purchased since that time. Here was the customer who had not left the neighborhood for more than seven days in living, byte-sized memory. Last spring, he'd tried—and failed—to cut down on patisseries and sugar. Today, for once, he had resisted his usual impulse purchase of a packet of cheroots.

Computer screened a message on the woman's till: Cheroots . . . Cheroots . . . it said. Remind the customer he has not purchased cereals or cheese or vegetables this month. Remind him of our *special offers*: 12 cans of lager for the price of 10. Buy one bottle of our Boulevard liqueur and get a second free. Remind him that time is passing more quickly than he thinks—his washing powder should be used by now, as should the contraceptives that he bought two years ago. He must need basics, such as rice and pasta, soap, toothpaste, flour, oil, and condiments. Inform him of our Retail Schemes and that we open now on Sunday afternoons. Advise him that he ought to do more cooking for himself. He ought to tidy up and clean the bathroom tiles with our new lemon whitener. He ought to start afresh. Suggest to him he tour our shelves again. At once. For what we choose is what we are. He should not miss this second opportunity to re-create himself with food.

GEOMETRY CAN FAIL US

Barbara Jacksha

Moments before the dead oak fell, we formed an equilateral triangle. In one corner, my new wife Sherri had been wielding the chain saw like a lumberjack, her black hair speckled with sawdust, her breath chuffing up steam. Now she stood behind the notched-out tree, feet braced, ready to push it forward toward the ice. Sherri's father, Buck, the north woods cowboy, barked orders from another corner of the triangle. Coatless, hatless, and thirty feet out on the lake, he locked his legs into a wide, bent-knee stance; his bare fingers gripped one of the ropes we'd looped high in the oak's limbs. At the third corner of the triangle, I waited — the shivering city boy — half listening to Buck while noticing things like positional geometry and the unfamiliar tightness of the second rope wound around my gloved hand. If felled right, the oak would tip straight forward, between Buck and me, chopping our perfect triangle in half.

Ice groaned beneath my feet. It was late in the season to be dropping a tree; the ice was already dark and slushy, and spring breakup could come at any time.

But Father knew best.

Buck waved his arm and shouted, "Go."

Sherri leaned into the tree. I pulled my rope hard. I grinned at Buck just as the rope slipped from his hands and slung through the air like a rodeo lasso. I decided I'd better toss my rope up too, but the oak was splitting, falling—not along that perfect, bisecting line, but directly at me.

I slipped off my rope-wrapped glove and ran, managing a half dozen lurching steps before I tripped. I pitched forward, skidded until my hands hit a knob of hard-packed snow. A few yards away, the oak smashed the ice. A branch scraped my leg. The tree shuddered as it hit bottom and lodged in the mud.

Elation zipped through me. I stood—victorious, alive—shouting "I'm fine" across a tangle of oak and a jagged pool of ice water roused from hibernation. I brushed off my legs; my calf was bleeding. When I looked for Sherri, my elation rattled off like vibrations through the ice. Sherri was no longer on the shore.

She'd run to her father's side. She clutched his arm; her wide eyes checked him for damage. Once she was satisfied, she finally looked in my direction. Her expression was a foreign, indecipherable language.

Then I realized that the equilateral image was gone: the triangle we now formed was undeniably acute. As Sherri jogged toward me, I looked away; I didn't want to watch her trace an awkward line toward the distant position I occupied—the narrow, sharp tip of the triangle, the puny outer angle squeezed almost to the vanishing point.

TO REDUCE YOUR LIKELIHOOD OF MURDER

Ander Monson

Do not go outside. Do not go outside, on dates, or to the store. Do not go on dates with men. Do not go on dates with men who drive. Do not drive yourself to dates, because that may anger the man you are dating who may wonder if you're too good to step foot in his new custom chrome *baby-baby* car. Do not date men who sit in or lean on cars. Do not sit in cars or sprawl yourself against the seat, or lean up against the metal skin of the door while you are being kissed. Do not date at night. Do not walk at night. Do not walk at night alone. Do not be alone. Walk with a girlfriend or someone else. A man you trust? Do not spend time with men, men friends, or boys. Do not spend time with any kind of men at all. Do not spend time with friends at all. Most women are killed by someone they know. Most women are killed by someone they know intimately.

Install alarm systems on every window, every doorway in your house. Better, do not live in a house. Go apartment. Go co-op. Go someplace where you can be heard, where someone can hear you scream. Do not venture out in public (at night, alone). Do not stay at home. Do not wear black. Do not wear the dress your boyfriend likes so much. Do not date your boyfriend whom you like so much. Do not like so much. Do not say *like* so much. Everyone is a potential murderer. And murderee. You are the murderee. You are single, seventeen, and thin. You are a thing made for television, for the nights of drama crime. Do not watch crime shows on TV or DVD. Do not open the door for anyone. Do not tell your mother that you don't know when you'll be back. Do not frustrate. Do not comply. You must lie somewhere in-between.

Do not sleep deeply.

Do carry mace, or pepper spray, or a bowie knife. Do carry guns if you can get them. A crossbow. A blowgun. Do subscribe to the *Shotgun News* and carry it wherever you go. It will be a totem, will keep you safe from harm. Armor yourself: plate mail, chain mail, studded leather armor. Helms and chain-link gloves. Keep away from the windows at all times. You must be surprising: Always travel in a crowd, in a cloud of smoke. Cover all your tracks. Keep an eye behind. Switch cabs. Duck into dead-end streets and wait for cars to pass.

Still you will be killed. You're born for it. Your life is a tree meant to be torn apart by weather and electricity.

OLIVER'S EVOLUTION

John Updike

His parents had not meant to abuse him; they had meant to love him, and did love him. But Oliver had come late in their little pack of offspring, at a time when the challenge of child-rearing was wearing thin, and he proved susceptible to mishaps. A big fetus, cramped in his mother's womb, he was born with in-turned feet, and learned to crawl with corrective casts up to his ankles. When they were at last removed, he cried in terror, because he thought those heavy plaster boots scraping and bump-ing along the floor had been part of himself.

One day in his infancy they found him on their dressing-room floor with a box of mothballs, some of which were wet with saliva; in retrospect they wondered if there had really been a need to rush him to the hospital and have his poor little stomach pumped. His face was gray-green afterwards. The following summer, when he had learned to walk, his parents had unthinkingly swum away off the beach together, striving for romantic harmony the morning after a late party and an alcoholic quarrel, and were quite unaware, until they saw the lifeguard racing along the beach, that Oliver had toddled after them and had been floating on his face for what might have been, given a less alert lifeguard, a fatal couple of minutes. This time, his face was blue, and he coughed for hours.

He was the least complaining of their children. He did not blame his parents when neither they nor the school authorities detected his "sleepy" right eye in time for therapy, with the result that when he closed that eye everything looked intractably fuzzy. Just the sight of the boy holding a schoolbook at a curious angle to the light made his father want to weep, impotently.

And it happened that he was just the wrong, vulnerable age when his parents went through their separation and divorce. His older brothers were off in boarding school and college, embarked on manhood, free of family. His younger sister was small enough to find the new arrangements—the meals in restaurants with her father, the friendly men who appeared to take her mother out— exciting. But Oliver, at thirteen, felt the weight of the household descend on him; he made his mother's sense of abandonment his own. Again, his father impotently grieved. It was he, and not the boy, who was at fault, really, when the bad grades began to come in from day school, and then from college, and Oliver broke his arm falling down the frat stairs, or leaping, by another account of the confused incident, from a girl's dormitory window. Not one but several family automobiles met a ruinous end with him at the wheel, though with no more injury, as it happened, than contused knees and loosened front teeth. The teeth grew firm again, thank God, for his innocent smile, slowly spreading across his face as the full humor of his newest misadventure dawned, was one of his best features. His teeth were small and round and widely spaced—baby teeth.

Then he married, which seemed yet another mishap, to go with the late nights, abandoned jobs, and fallen-through opportunities of his life as a young adult. The girl, Alicia, was as accident-prone as he, given to substance abuse and unwanted pregnancies. Her emotional disturbances left herself and others bruised. By comparison, Oliver was solid and surefooted, and she looked up to him. This was the key. What we expect of others, they endeavor to provide. He held on to a job, and she held on to her pregnancies. You should see him now, with their two children, a fair little girl and a dark-haired boy. Oliver has grown broad, and holds the two of them at once. They are birds in a nest. He is a tree, a sheltering boulder. He is a protector of the weak.

THE DOCTOR

Ann Hood

The doctor who killed my father wants to take me for coffee. *Starbucks,* he says. *The Coffee Café. Java Man.* He gives me options. He tells me he wants to talk about my father's treatment, his cancer, how hard he tried to save his life. *I didn't kill him,* he always says. *I just couldn't save him.* The distinction is lost on me. After all, I'm the one who had to walk into my father's room every day, grinning, lighthearted. I'm the one who had to explain about metastasizing, lymph nodes, Taxol; my father was a welder, a man who read *Reader's Digest* on the toilet and sometimes the Sunday paper. He did not really know what was out there.

The doctor who killed my father is as handsome as an Italian movie star: dark curly hair and a droopy handlebar mustache. He is from Chicago. He is divorced. He sees his kids every other weekend and alternating holidays. I learned all this during the long weeks of my father's illness. *Won't see you this weekend*, he'd say. *Got my kids.* While I tried to get my father to drink his Ensure, I would imagine the doctor at their soccer games or buying them Happy Meals.

Even though I was falling in love with the doctor, I hated him, too. My father wasn't an every-other-weekend-and-alternating-holidays father. He drove me to school each morning, stopping at Dunkin' Donuts for Bavarian creams. He nursed me through measles, chicken pox, my tonsillectomy. He moved me from apartment to apartment, from broken heart to broken heart. He was a guy who was always around. Sometimes I would watch the doctor from my father's hospital room window as he walked across the parking lot to his red station wagon. *Il Dottore*, I would think. The doctor. The doctor who can't help.

The next time he calls, it's a Saturday evening that fall, five months after my father died. I am standing at my kitchen sink, staring at the neighbor's elaborate jack-o'-lanterns. A witch on a broomstick and a frightened cat that seems to leap out of the pumpkin, poised in midair. My other neighbor has lined her back porch with luminaries: paper bags with lit votives inside. In fact, my entire neighborhood is glowing. Except for my house.

"How about an espresso with sambuca?" the doctor asks me. "We could go to Lucinda's? Do you know it?"

His house, like mine, is quiet.

"I know it," I say.

When I was not with someone, my father was my Saturday-night date. We used to go for barbecue ribs, or lobster dinners. We used to share a bottle of wine, a pitcher of beer.

"I didn't kill him," the doctor is saying in a voice so low I can barely hear him.

"I know," I say again.

That morning of the day my father died, the doctor grabbed my arm hard. *I have tried everything,* he told me. *And still your father is going to die.* And I said, *Try something else. Do you hear me?* He shook his head. *We've run out of options.*

The doctor sighs. He laughs awkwardly, relieved. "You do see it then. It's an insidious disease. Horrible."

Darkness has fallen in that quick way it does this time of year. I am alone.

"Please," the doctor says, and he sounds eager, needy. "I would like to see you again. Under different circumstances. Better ones."

He was right about everything. The chances for survival, the progress of the disease, my father's inescapable death. But I do not want him to have everything. He can't lose my father and win the girl, too.

"No. I'm really not interested. Please don't keep calling."

When I hang up, I reach for the can that is sitting on the counter. It opens with a sigh. I set up the coffee maker for one cup. As it brews, I watch the glow of the tiny red light, waiting to hear the almost imperceptible click that tells me it is time.

CRAZY GLUE

Etgar Keret

She said, "Don't touch that."

"What is it?" I asked.

"It's glue," she said. "Special glue. The best kind."

"What did you buy it for?"

"Because I need it," she said. "A lot of things around here need gluing."

"Nothing around here needs gluing," I said. "I wish I understood why you buy all this stuff."

"For the same reason I married you," she murmured. "To help pass the time."

I didn't want to fight, so I kept quiet, and so did she.

"Is it any good, this glue?" I asked. She showed me the picture on the box, with this guy hanging upside down from the ceiling.

"No glue can really make a person stick like that," I said. "They just took the picture upside down. They must have put a light fixture on the floor." I took the box from her and peered at it. "And there, look at the window. They didn't even bother to hang the blinds the other way. They're upside down, if he's really standing on the ceiling. Look," I said again, pointing to the window. She didn't look.

"It's eight already," I said. "I've got to run." I picked up my briefcase and kissed her on the cheek "I'll be back pretty late. I'm working—"

"Overtime," she said. "Yes, I know."

I CALLED ABBY from the office.

"I can't make it today," I said. "I've got to get home early."

"Why?" Abby asked. "Something happen?"

"No . . . I mean, maybe. I think she suspects something."

There was a long silence. I could hear Abby's breathing on the other end.

"I don't see why you stay with her," she whispered. "You never do anything together. You don't even fight. I'll never understand it." There was a pause, and then she repeated, "I wish I understood." She was crying.

"I'm sorry. I'm sorry, Abby. Listen, someone just came in," I lied. "I've got to hang up. I'll come over tomorrow. I promise. We'll talk about everything then."

I GOT HOME EARLY. I said "Hi" as I walked in, but there was no reply. I went through all the rooms in the house. She wasn't in any of them. On the kitchen table I found the tube of glue, completely empty. I tried to move one of the chairs, to sit down. It didn't budge. I tried again. Not an inch. She'd glued it to the floor. The fridge wouldn't open. She'd glued it shut. I didn't understand what was happening, what would make her do such a thing. I didn't know where she was. I went into the living room to call her mother's. I couldn't lift the receiver; she'd glued that too. I kicked the table and almost broke my toe. It didn't even budge.

And then I heard her laughing. It was coming from somewhere above me. I looked up, and there she was, standing barefoot on the living room ceiling.

I stared openmouthed. When I found my voice I could only ask, "What the hell . . . are you out of your mind?"

She didn't answer, just smiled. Her smile seemed so natural, with her hanging upside down like that, as if her lips were just stretching on their own by the sheer force of gravity.

"Don't worry, I'll get you down," I said, hurrying to the shelf and grabbing the largest books. I made a tower of encyclopedia volumes and clambered on top of the pile.

"This may hurt a little," I said, trying to keep my balance. She went on smiling. I pulled as hard as I could, but nothing happened. Carefully, I climbed down.

"Don't worry," I said. "I'll get the neighbors or something. I'll go next door and call for help."

"Fine," she laughed. "I'm not going anywhere."

I laughed too. She was so pretty, and so incongruous, hanging upside down from the ceiling that way. With her long hair dangling downwards, and her breasts molded like two perfect teardrops under her white T-shirt. So pretty. I climbed back up onto the pile of books and kissed her. I felt her tongue on mine. The books tumbled out from under my feet, but I stayed floating in midair, hanging just from her lips.

PLEDGE DRIVE

Patricia Marx

You were just listening to an uninterrupted hour of Patty, featuring some catty remarks about her best friends. Isn't Patty fantastic? They simply don't make them like Patty anymore. And that's why it's so important to make sure that she continues to be the person you know and love. But Patty can't do that alone. That's where you come in. At least we hope so. We'll be back with Patty talking about her hair in a little while, but right now we want to take a few moments to remind you how much Patty did for you this year.

You've come to rely on Patty to provide you with information you can't get anywhere else. A report on what she had for lunch. The latest on her trying to return a magnifying glass without a store receipt. Whom else can you turn to for news about Patty's day?

Your other friends give you sound bites, but Patty takes the time to fill in the details about things like the time she got lost in New Jersey. You simply can't get that level of quality discourse with anyone else, because most people have things to do. Did you know that the average phone conversation you have with Patty lasts twelve minutes and you're usually the one who hangs up first?

Think about it. Patty has affected your life in immeasurable ways. You've become accustomed to a bounty of e-mails from Patty, some of them jokes or petitions that Patty has forwarded along without reading first.

Or maybe you've only sat next to Patty on the bus or at the theatre, not having any idea who Patty was but grateful that she wasn't somebody else. If you were trying to read Patty's newspaper, didn't Patty let you? And how about the time Patty was using her bank card to gain access to the A.T.M., and even though she knew you were sneaking in behind her so as to get out of scrounging around for your own card, Patty made no fuss?

Aren't these services worth a lot to you?

As of three years ago, Patty was totally dependent on parental funding. When that support was cut off, it was touch and go whether Patty would be able to survive another year. A lot of people you know have jobs, but, in order to preserve Patty's dignity, Patty has declined to work, and so she must count on pledges from friends like you. (Every once in a while, a nice gentleman treats Patty to dinner, but you can't expect her to live off that, can you?)

Patty's operating expenses have gone up and up—never more so than this year, because the cost of fancy skin creams, designer leather jackets, and other essential goods has risen disproportionately to the rate of inflation. And Patty really wants to go to Istanbul in April.

I'm not going to tell you how much to give, but I am going to tell you that Patty keeps the book on who gives what. Perhaps you'd like to give at the $10,000 level. Over the course of a year, this is only $27.39 per day—the same amount of money you run through for your daily eight lattes without thinking twice. For just $200, you can underwrite one of Patty's sessions with Dr. Cates. Throw in an extra $50 and Patty will spend the entire fifty minutes working bravely on her issues involving you. But perhaps you can't afford that amount. At the $50 level, you can . . . oh, forget it. Fifty bucks?! You've got to be kidding!

When you become a contributor, with a pledge of $100 or more you may select a thank-you gift from Patty. For instance, do you need any clothes hangers? And if you act right away you can also get a magnifying glass with an undetectable chip. Or, for a donation of $500, Patty will blow you.

So what's stopping you? Call now. Patty is standing by to take your money. Talk to your accountant: Patty could be a write-off. And, if you'd like to volunteer to help out on the phone bank, please do. You'll get to meet Patty in person. She's got bagels!

THE HANDBAG

Michael Augustin

translated from the German by Sujata Bhatt

A certain Blunk, who has made a name for himself as a professional thief of handbags, finds himself, on the occasion of one of his assaults, confronted with eighty-two-year-old Elisabeth Schröder, whose handbag he intends to snatch by applying the usual quick, powerful jerking motion.

Now, what frequently happens in this situation is that elderly ladies, out of sheer fright, forget to release their grip and thus are pulled to the ground, whereupon they invariably acquire a fracture of the upper part of a thighbone before they finally let go of the strap and the robber, who then runs away.

Completely different, however, is the case with eighty-two-year-old Elisabeth Schröder. It doesn't even occur to her to let go of the handbag. As a consequence Blunk is compelled to drag the old lady behind him, through the bushes, diagonally across the extensive lawns of the park, yes, through the entire inner city, straight into a commuter bus and right out again, for hours on end, until Blunk, who is really quite a strong and athletic young man, can barely continue due to exhaustion, and so finally has to come to a standstill, right in the middle of the street.

This, of course, is the moment that eighty-two-year-old Elisabeth Schröder has been waiting for. In a jiffy she bounces back to her feet, and now it's her turn to drag the horrified Blunk behind her until she is so tired she can't anymore, and then it's his turn again.

This has been going on for three years now and everyone thinks that there's something sweet cooking between the two of them.

A PATRIOTIC ANGEL

Mark Budman

She stands in the supermarket aisle reserved for the holiday decorations. She is not tall; maybe five inches maximum. She wears a regulation angel's gown and a red, white and blue scarf about her shoulders in the manner of a priest or a Reform rabbi. She holds a tiny harp, but she doesn't play it yet.

"What will you play for me?" Len asks, bending down to her. "'The Star-Spangled Banner'? 'Silent Night'? A Hanukkah song?" His left hip hurts, but he wants to make sure she hears him well.

"Are you working here?" he continues. "Or did they lay you off, too? . . . Stupid question. Of course you are working here. As an angel."

He touches the strings of her harp with his finger. They sigh.

"I've never seen your kind before. Only everyday, down-to-earth angels . . . What makes you what you are? Do you fly with our pilots to protect them in a battle? Or maybe you advise our government officials and American company CEOs?"

Her plastic fingers move. She plays a few notes from "America the Beautiful." His hip can't stand it any longer. He sits on the floor. Now their faces are on the same level.

"I've always been a patriot. Voted. Paid taxes. Even served a stint in Vietnam. We are alike, you and I. We could be friends."

A woman pushes a cart by him. She meets Len's eyes and purses her lips. He turns to the angel again. "If I take you home, I would have to leave the steak, grapes, beer and the cereal here. You might be bored at my place; my kids are already in college, and my wife is always at work."

Her eyes say, "Why do I care?" Or, perhaps, "Sure, Daddy."

Outside, the first snowflakes of the night land on his baseball cap. He will listen to five patriotic songs tonight, playing in the sequence of his choice, in the company of an angel while drinking milk and eating bread. What more can a man possibly want?

WHAT WERE THE WHITE THINGS?

Amy Hempel

These pieces of crockery are a repertory company, playing roles in each dream. No, that's not the way it started. He said the pieces of crockery play roles in each *painting*. The artist clicked through slides of still lifes he had painted over thirty years. Someone in the small, attentive audience said, "Isn't that the cup in the painting from years ago?" Yes, it was, the artist said, and the pitcher and mixing bowl and goblet, too. Who was the nude woman leaning against the table on which the crockery was displayed? The artist didn't say, and no one in the small, attentive audience asked.

I was content to look at objects that had held the attention of a gifted man for so many years. I arrived at the lecture on my way to someplace else, an appointment with a doctor my doctor had arranged. Two days before, she was telling me his name and address and I have to say, I stopped listening, even though—or because—it was important. So instead of going to the radiologist's office, I walked into a nondenominational church where the artist's presentation was advertised on a plaque outside: "Finding the Mystery in Clarity." Was this not the opposite of what most people sought? I thought, I will learn something!

The crockery was white, not glazed, and painted realistically. The pieces threw different lengths of shadows depending on the angle of the light in each painting. Sometimes the pieces were lined up touching one another, and other times there were gaps. Were these gaps part of the mystery the artist had in mind? Did he mean for us to be literal, to think: absence? He said the mind wants to make sense of a thing, the mind wants to know what something stands for. Okay, the artist said, here is what I painted that September. On the screen, we saw a familiar tabletop—objects familiar from years of his still lifes—and the two tallest pieces of crockery, the pitcher and the vase, were missing; nothing stood in their places.

Ahhhh, the small, attentive audience said. .

Then someone asked the artist, What were the white things? He meant what were the white things in the other paintings. What did they represent? And the artist said that was not a question he would answer.

My mother, near the end of her life, announced that she was giving everything away. She was enraged. She told me to put a sticker on anything I wanted to keep, but every time I did, she said she had promised the thing to someone else. The house was all the houses I had grown up in. The things I wanted to keep were all white. But what *were* the white things?

After the lecture, I tried to remember what I had wanted to keep. But all I could say was that the things I wanted to keep were white.

After the lecture, a call to my doctor's receptionist, and I had the address of the specialist. I wasn't so late that he wouldn't see me.

When the films were developed, an assistant brought them into the examination room. The doctor placed them up against lights and pointed out the distinct spots he said my doctor had suspected he would find. I told him I would have thought the spots would be dark. I said, Is this not what most people would expect?

The doctor told me the meaning of what we looked at on the film. He asked me if I understood what he said. I said yes. I said yes, and that I wanted to ask one question: What were the white things?

The doctor said he would explain it to me again, and proceeded to tell me a second time. He asked me if this time I understood what he had told me. Yes, I said. I said, Yes, but what were the white things?

MAP OF THE LOST WORLD

James Tate

Things were getting to me, things of no consequence in themselves, but taken together, they were undermining my ability to cope. I needed a hammer to nail something up, but my hammer wasn't in the toolbox. It wasn't anywhere to be found. I broke a dish while putting away the dishes, but where's the broom? Not in the broom closet. How do you lose a broom? Where was it hiding? And, then, later, while making the bed, I found the hammer. Perhaps it was used as a sleeping-aid device. Then Kelly called and said she had lost her ring last night and would I please look under the bed. I looked and found the broom there. So I decided to sweep under there to see if I could find her ring. I swept out a rosary, a spark plug, a snakeskin—three feet long—, a copy of *Robert's Rules of Order*, a swizzle stick, a jawbreaker, and much more. But no ring. I put the broom into the broom closet, and started to feel a little better. I hung the picture and put the hammer into the toolbox. I made myself a cup a tea, and sat down in the living room. I had no idea how any of that stuff could have gotten under my bed. None of it belonged to me. It was quite a disturbing assortment. Then I thought of Kelly's ring, and how it could have fallen behind one of the cushions on the couch. I drank some tea to calm my nerves. I drank some more tea. Then I lifted up the first cushion. There was about three dollars' worth of change and a monkey carved out of teak. I didn't like the monkey at all, but I was happy to have the three dollars. Under the next cushion there was a small glass hand, a lead soldier in a gas mask, a key ring with three keys, and a map of Frankfurt, Germany. I sipped my tea. My hands were shaking. The whole morning was frittering away with nonsense. I had work to do, or, if not that, then I should be relaxing. I wasn't going to look under the third cushion, and I wasn't going to look for Kelly's ring anymore at all. I sat there without moving, my mind drifting over the clouds. I was pulling a yak over a mountaintop, hauling water and rice to a dead wise man, who knows nothing, says nothing.

BILL

Dan Kaplan

In a frayed wool sweater, Bill with a sword splitting a coconut FedExed from Hawaii. Bill perched on a barstool, joints throbbing, rain pounding the tin roof. *The Wizard of Oz* on Bill's black-and-white set. Bill thrown to the pavement. The sun, as though shot into the sky from Bill's finger. A woman whispering "Bill" to herself, divvying the dog-eared paperbacks. Bill asking the couple to sit down, their faces uncommitted. The highway unspooling, Bill reclining. Someone screaming "Cedric!" from across the street in a new town. Red-eared, pelted by hail, Bill studying the numbers on the house. Bill's hairless cat, sunburned, found in the gutter by another kid. The book of baby names left open at the V's. Bill tipping a thick-thighed female impersonator with an outstretched garter. A gaunt physician, two years from retiring, handing Bill a prescription. Bill giving a last over-the-shoulder look. Two o'clock appointment with Bill scratched out on the calendar. "Bill" stitched in cursive red letters on the breast pocket of a shirt worn by a teenager who never knew Bill. A woman Bill hardly knows opening the front door. The two-person bathtub in which Bill once had three people. Bill on a first visit to the ward, scanning the list on the wall. Bill's picture of a tearful Pope in drag accepting the Miss Universe crown. Bill, cold. The moon like a butter pat in the southern sky. A line winding around the corner, Bill near the end. Bill seeing an ad for something called "yoga." Someone screaming "Bill!" in the terminal, everyone looking.

THE KETTLE

Eva Marie Ginsburg

In truth, the pot never called the kettle black. It never spoke to the kettle directly. Nor did any of the pots, but every time the kettle whistled, they expressed their disgust by turning slightly toward one another, shifting a handle up, or rattling their disapproval. None of them liked the kettle. It had a soft black finish, like charcoal, and a very queer asymmetrical handle, white plastic with maddening black lines that came in varying widths and ran in different directions. It had been designed by some prestigious Swedish artist whose name nobody knew how to pronounce. It was supposed to look very modern and dramatic, but everybody knows pots and kettles are for cooking in, not for looking at, and the pots liked to jeer at it. They ridiculed it with rattles and bumps. They muttered behind its back. They scoffed and they tittered, and sometimes, next to it on the stove, they gleefully splattered the kettle with grease. They could all tell from the lines on its handle and the way its spout stuck out, calling attention to itself, that the kettle considered itself more important than the others. And then there was the matter of its whistle, the way it screamed when it boiled and got louder and louder until the man came to turn it off—as though the kettle believed the man existed to serve it, and not the other way around. The very idea of the whistle outraged them. Besides, to add insult to injury, the kettle had been given to him by the woman.

That the woman never came around anymore changed nothing. They knew all about it, knew how the kettle had been bought at an expensive store and wrapped up in December with pretty paper and a ribbon, and had been presented along with some extra-large mugs and loose luxury tea leaves. The pots knew all about it, how the man and woman had eaten the stuffed chicken breasts and the apricot couscous and finished the bottle of red wine, and the pleasure they'd had. The pots told themselves it didn't matter, that they were more important because the man had bought them himself, with money that he earned those nights he came home too late and too tired to cook. They were capable of cooking so many things, soup and fried rice and pasta and chocolate mousse, but the kettle was only good for boiling water, something any one of them could have done.

They couldn't forget, though, that night the woman had brought the kettle, the meal and the wine and the candles she lit around the house, and the way the man sang to himself after she left. They despised the kettle, but secretly they envied it, even though the woman had been gone for many months now, even though the pretty box had been thrown away and the man cooked more simply these days and had stopped singing softly in the kitchen. They were beginning to tire of mocking the kettle. They wished they had a sweeter way to pass the time.

QUILL

Tony Earley

As Thompson stared at Quill, the oxygen tube protruding from Quill's nostrils, curving up and back over his cheeks, took on the appearance of tusks; Quill's immaculate brush cut swept back from his widow's peak in a broad, white stripe; when he frowned he looked fierce.

"What?" Quill said. "What do you think you're looking at?"

"I just realized," said Thompson, "that, with that thing sticking out of your nose, you look like a pig."

"That's a hell of a thing to say," said Quill. "To come in here, to come into intensive care and tell a man in my condition, to tell a man with a *heart* condition, that he looks like a pig."

"A *wild* pig," Thompson said. "A boar. A big old wild boar."

"If I get up out of this chair."

"Full of piss."

"You've had the lick now, boy."

"And vinegar. With a big old pork pecker. A big old pork pecker dragging through the leaves. Digging a ditch through the woods. You could lay pipe in it. Balls like mushmelons."

"You," said Quill. His eyes closed and he opened them again. "Have always been full of it."

Thompson grinned. Remembered a Sunday in 1946. Fall. School clothes. Shoes. Quill would not get off the bicycle. He rode around and around the yard. Thompson yelled, Quill! It's my turn! Quill threw back his head and brayed the Lone Ranger song. *Da da duh. Da da duh. Da da duh duh DUH!* Thompson picked up an apple, a horse apple big as a softball, and let it fly. It caught Quill in the ear. Bad wreck. Quill climbed out from under the bike, the rear wheel still spinning, and tried to beat the dirt off his shirt; he was always funny about his clothes. Thompson could hear him breathing all the way across the yard. I know what I'll do, Quill said. I'll just kill you. Thompson lit out across the pasture; Quill sprinted for the house and the gun. The hackberry tree seemed a mile or more away. Thompson panted, Tree, Tree, Tree, Tree, while he ran. He heard the screen door bang open. Thompson dove behind the tree. Quill shot the whole tube. Eighteen rounds. Thompson heard the bullets slapping into the wood. Then it was over. Quill threw down the rifle and ran across the pasture. He brushed off Thompson's clothes. Cried and kissed Thompson all over the face. Told him how much he loved him, how sorry he was. Thompson didn't feel anything at all. He wasn't mad. He wasn't afraid. Nothing. They buried the shell casings behind the barn.

"Quill," Thompson said, "you remember that time you tried to kill me?"

Quill blinked. His eyes grew indistinct, as if sinking behind a surface of bright water. The water in each eye squeezed itself into a ball and rolled down his cheeks until the oxygen tube stopped it like a dam. "I tried to shoot you, Teenie," he said. "I tried to shoot my little brother."

"You missed me," said Thompson. "You missed me, Quill. Hey."

Quill began to sob. "And now I'm going to die, Teenie. I tried to shoot my little brother, and now I'm going to die."

Thompson glanced up at Quill's monitor.

"They said I've got damage. Teenie, they said part of my heart is dead."

Quill's hands were soft and warm. Thompson could feel *that*, although when he looked at his own hands they did not seem part of him. He stared at them as if they belonged to a stranger. He thought, on purpose, Quilly. My Quilly. My big Quilly is dying, but could not produce a single tear. He thought, Cry, Jesus, please let me cry, but what he said was, "Quill. Seriously. You cannot shoot. Worth. A. Lick."

NICARAGUA

Kirk Nesset

What you leave out, describing it all, is the girl. How pretty she was—petite, exquisitely cheekboned, Norwegian. The way she bumped your shoulder with hers in the dark as you walked toward the lake. A walk, you thought, was the appropriate move. You don't say to nice girls in hotels, even down there, in Spanish less polished than hers, Want to adjourn to my room? The fact is the lake after dark is not safe. You didn't know. Or didn't know what you knew.

What you leave out is everything. The lovely near-perfect Spanish with its Scandinavian lilt. The world dropping parcel by parcel away in the pastel candlelit bar. Her delicate chin, cheeks sprinkled with freckles. The story you tell is bare action, assailants gliding from shadows, surreal. Why dwell on what happened after?

She came to your room and you sat in shock, bed to bed, talking. Inert you remained, sans passport, sans bank checks, plastic and cash, no coins even to get a cab to the cop station. Why regret what you might have done and did not? Like lie down beside her, attempt the comfort that nearness might bring?

What you leave out is why you went to Nicaragua at all. You don't really know. All you know—later—is that you bottomed out there in intricate ways. Robbery was merely the ostensible way, the part that most palpably grates.

The *calle*, the city, the very country grows progressively nasty, more filthy, desperate, each time you tell it. The number of assailants increases. They're men now, not boys, each armed with a knife. In truth you saw only one blade. The girl didn't see any.

PARROT TALK

Kit Coyne Irwin

There's not much to tell, the squawks made me look up, and in the tree are these gigantic nests, the size of sofas. An intricate mesh of sticks and whatnot woven around a tree limb. Like the second Little Pig's house—his tree house, like a wooden cocoon. I jog around the tree, watching, waiting to see the bird that can build this nest. But it's the bird's shadow I see first as it flies over my head. Sizable, but not enormous. Twirled about, I see the bird perched high in the tree. A brilliant green. The size of a starling. A parrot? In Connecticut?

At dinner that night, I tell my husband about the parrot I saw while jogging. His words echo my earlier thoughts exactly, "A parrot? In Connecticut?" It's part of the synchronicity that exists between married people. The same synchronicity that allows me to hear his next words before he says them. "Don't be ridiculous!"

At a party that weekend, my husband tells my story of seeing the parrot. He makes the bird a flock and me a complete idiot.

I don't tell anyone else about the parrot. I change my jogging route. Can't give up jogging—jogging reduces stress. But I still see the parrots (there's more than one now), flying overhead, perched in trees, eating at feeders. These birds don't chirp, peep, twitter, tweet, trill, warble, nor sing. For them, only loud calls of demand.

On Thursday, I don't drive my husband to the train station, I take him to see the parrots. Beneath the oak tree, under the nests, I park our car and say, "Let them shit on us." Our synchronicity is broken, I don't know what he will say.

In a sarcastic tone, he says, "The birds are pretty. I've seen them. Let's go." Not a novel response, but I surprise myself—I parrot back his words. "The birds are pretty. I've seen them. Let's go." It annoys him; it would annoy me. Especially as I keep repeating everything he says, and when we get to the cut-that-out's and the I-mean-it's, I think he's going to hit me. I am disappointed when he just gets out of the car and heads towards the next train.

There used to be a time when we said, "I love you," back and forth, back and forth. Whose turn is it now? I run after him and yell, "Wait up." He repeats, "Wait up."

But I know how to beat him at the parrot game. "I'm sorry. I love you."

Silence. I repeat myself and then say, "Goddamn it, I said I love you."

He repeats, "Goddamn it," until we reach the train station. Fine with me. Beside him, I chime in, "Goddamn it." I'm going to goddamn-it into New York City with him. Perhaps he senses that, because instead of getting on the train, he asks, "What do you want?"

I do not know how to answer that. You can't ask someone to love you, can you?

He says, "Let's find out what kind of goddamn birds those are."

The ornithologist from the local university tells us they are indeed parrots, escaped from the zoo over fifteen years ago, seven of them, now there's over a thousand, amazing how they have adapted to a hostile environment, how they even flourish.

I DIDN'T DO THAT

Tom Hazuka

I look for a smile. I feel it in his words: "Sex and violence don't mix. Why waste good violence on sex?" But Roger—my best friend as a kid, best man at my wedding six years ago—is concentrating too hard to smile. He's staring down the barrel of his 30.06, waiting for that snapping turtle to stick his head above water again. He doesn't want it eating the game fish in his pond. I've seen him shoot half a dozen since junior high.

"I never hit her," he says evenly. "I never hit her even once."

"Of course you didn't," I say.

"I don't know what makes her say that, Jimmy."

Roger never uses Carla's name since she left. But she's not a "cheating bitch" or "worthless whore" either, like some other friends' ex-wives—or my own, once or twice, when pain won out over pride.

"Come on, don't worry about it. No one believes her." The lie feels like dirt on my tongue.

I like Carla. She's smart, and secure enough about it that even in high school she didn't play dumb. One time she told me of a nightmare Roger had, over ten years after he got back from Vietnam. He was writhing on his stomach, she said, whimpering over and over *Burning people smell so bad* without waking up.

"I didn't dare touch him," she said. She put her hand on my arm. "You're the only one I've told this to. Not even him." Carla stared off at nothing, nodding slowly. She shrugged. "Especially not him."

Roger's finger is tight on the trigger. Suddenly he looks away from his target, straight at me.

"Remember when we were kids, and we found that dead bullfrog on the other side of the pond? Nailed down on a stump?"

I nod. I can still see that spread-eagled frog, belly-up and leathery black from the sun, its gut a squirming ball of maggots. It gave me nightmares for a week.

Roger takes aim again, out across the water. "I didn't do that," he says.

WHAT I KNOW OF YOUR COUNTRY

John Leary

Did you know in your country, in the state of Ohio, there is a man whose name is "R. A. All Beef O'Myers?" The evidence is here on my KallService Ltd. Call Sheet. I know that in your country it is unusual for people to have names that are nouns. I have been doing my job for four months here at KallService.

I also know that the dinner hour in an American household is a sacred time. I know this because one of your countrymen told this to me recently: "this is a sacred time." I had suspected this fact, because many times the Christian god had been invoked to damn me for having called at such an hour.

Many of you like to talk. I find this when I call sometimes, there are women who want to talk to me, who ask me my name, who say I have a "nice voice." I had two weeks of KallService Ltd.

training to disguise my accent. KallService Ltd. assigns the name "Kenny" to the occupant of this cubicle. I say my name is Kenny. When women ask my location, the KallService manual instructs me that I must decline to say anything. However if sometimes I am pressed and the woman has a nice voice too, I will lie and say "Nebraska" because I feel strongly the touch of the word in my mouth. My current residence is in truth here in Chandigarh, though it is not the town of my birth.

I am responsible for the area in the middle of your country, the rectangular states.

Two days ago I called a household and asked for the head of household and the man who answered told me to wait a moment. Through the receiver I could hear people laughing, there seemed to be many people laughing. A man named Raymond was speaking and people were laughing even though the things he was saying did not seem humorous. Then all of the people in the room sang a song about beer, then a woman discussed the fact that some men might want to see their doctor in order to begin really living again. My call-clock reached zero, so I had to terminate the phone call. I am humbled to admit that it was only shortly before terminating the call that I realized I had been listening to the television.

During many calls, children in the background cry and screech, just as in my country.

Another thing I know is that many people in your country are bold, like explorers or inventors. Sometimes the boldness may seem to new employees of KallService Ltd. to be rude. I explain that you know and I know that if you were to spend but a brief few minutes with me discussing your long-distance calling plan, by the end of the call I would have found a way to save you money. And yet many Americans do not even have the time to talk to me? That is another example of your boldness, your confidence, your abundance.

The KallService Ltd. manual does not tell trainees about the women of your country. My colleagues and I know that many people in your country live alone. Many of these people living alone are women. I know when I have reached the house of an alone person because there is a certain weight to the silence behind them, or the volume of the stereo music or television will be falsely loud. The women in these empty domiciles often want to talk beyond the limits of my call-clock. They seem very interested in a man like me. I have been here at KallService Ltd. for four months, and next month I will join my cousin in his solid-soup business. But now I have more days sitting in my cubicle calling the women of your country. I listen and try to hear in their voice the sights they are seeing outside their windows. Outside their windows are fields of wheat, white-crowned mountains, the Grand Canyon, or the Statute of Liberty. Some day I will travel to your rectangular states. From the window you will see me, coming to the front door. You will offer me a lemonade, and I will tell you I have come from Nebraska.

THE PAPERBOY

Sherrie Flick

I seduced the paperboy yesterday. It was slow and awkward, but I knew as soon as I got that thick sagging sack uncrossed from his shoulders—as soon as I got him settled on the far end of the couch—I had him.

The boy's mouth was smiling, I gave him a drink. Milk. It was what he wanted. He still smiled and I thought, he is the smallest bird. I touched his hair, his knee, his arm.

I call this flirting.

So soft and sweet, his lips opened to mine. He was speaking words I strained to hear, but my heart was in the way—just pounding.

It went like this: some hands moving, a kicking leg with a loose tube sock on the end, a silk shirt. A zipper. I swear he chirped.

He said I love you.

I love you; he said that. I told him to dress, to leave, to change his route. I handed him his bag weighed down still with neatly rolled papers, each banded with a rubber band, each placed in a thin plastic sheath with care and diligence. I walked to my window, put my back to him. I lit a cigarette. A strange drizzle had started — rain falling down through late afternoon sun.

I know my back. It is straight and narrow. I was making sure my life would be straight and long. I am much shyer and soft-spoken than I seem.

The boy shut my door softly with a click. He walked past the window, his untied boots flopping like lazy dying fish as he trudged down my walk. He looked then and waved — a slight boyish wave as if his mother had just reminded him to be polite. I watched him go. His aim was good. He got every porch square-on, the paper hitting the front door with a bang then rolling gently onto the welcome mat. The last rays of sun turned the corner with the boy; the street turned quickly into soft sleek grayness. A black dog trotted from one side to the other. A truck flashed its two red brake lights then signaled left.

I imagined the boy as he got older. I knew someday he too would be unkind. Perhaps he would start to understand how unkindnesses could be helpful, how people could be complex, how life could surprise you unless you told it what to do.

I make tea and sit at my table in my dim kitchen. The clock hums diligently above the refrigerator. Birds chirp off in the distance. I glance at my salt and pepper shakers on the stove, on the table, on the counter beside the sink. I know I have too many. I have too many dishes, too many pots and pans. I have too many books, and I've had too many men. I drink too much tea, but no one has told me to stop.

The phone rings. It rings again. It rings until halfway through it stops. I smile. I finger the spoon in the sugar bowl. I think about sweeteners—how there are so many and I have only this one kind sitting quietly on my table. I begin to see that this could be a problem. I start a shopping list that includes molasses, honey, and brown sugar.

He will tell his friends I took him like a movie star—that I was like a movie star from some old movie—so beautiful and graceful that I lit a cigarette afterwards and that the smoke curled upwards in this certain way he couldn't describe. He will say I wore dark lipstick and nothing else against my fair skin. He'll say I begged for more. He will smile coyly while he tells this story in the boys' bathroom. He will lean against the slick tile wall with his thin hands in his jeans pockets, with his ankles crossed. Every so often he will twitch his head to throw his hair out of his eyes. No one will believe him and soon even he will start to wonder what it was that happened to him over here in my dusty living room. Soon I will haunt his dreams in this way where I am barely recognizable— where I peek softly around the corner then turn before he can catch a glimpse of my face. He will never forget me. I will be the first woman he ever loved.

BIRTH

Robert Earle

Somehow their marriage got caught in the car engine and it blew up. First it ground to a halt, then it smoked, then came the fire and the explosion. The explosion was a muffled thud, a sound like a sack of cement or maybe an overstuffed chair pushed out a window and landing in an alley. She felt the thud drifting into her chest as she stood on the soft shoulder and then she saw it illuminate Hal's face with a purple powdery light, a light full of recrimination.

She had made the car do this.

The first day of vacation and the car was dead and now they were in this emotional alley, scattering their stuff everywhere as they pulled it out of the car and threw it behind them and saved it from the fire which caught her long hair on the right side of her face as she was grabbing at a canvas bag of crackers and magazines. *Poof!* Her hair just went up. Went up like tinder. Went up like a curtain.

She backed out of the car, caught her jacket on the window handle, looked at Hal for help, and saw in his crushed-can face the reflection of her head half on fire and half not.

He laughed.

It was a funny thing, this deadly laugh. The laugh was full of hate, and it ended their marriage, but it was the richest, most intimate and revealing sound he had made in three years of bedrooms and bathrooms and kitchens together. If he weren't laughing at her and hating the failure of their marriage and riding this awful sound away like some kind of magic carpet, he could have had her with it all over again. She would not have succumbed to it. Nothing like that. But she would have danced with this man and squeezed him and tried to get him to make some other gorgeous, powerful, wicked sounds out of sheer, perverse sexual fascination.

But her perversion was all used up.

And her head was on fire, so she stuck it in the canvas bag and fell down and rolled on the ground until the fire went out. Then she just lay there awhile, gasping.

Well, she could imagine him saying, this vacation is over. He would be bitter but relieved. Not going on vacation had its advantages. There would be work he could do at home, TV programs he could watch, and money he would not spend.

And normally she would have (had the marriage not already ended just like the vacation) argued just the opposite. She would have concocted some way to go on. These getaways were crucial.

But not this time, no. Crucial, but in a different sense.

The countryside around them had collapsed into this valley. She just sat there a bit. The sounds he was making weren't really words and she wasn't really hearing them and she didn't really care.

The people who stopped to help loaded them up in their van and drove them deeper into the valley where they found a hotel and she found, though it was late Saturday afternoon, a hair salon where a man and a woman working together carefully put her right. It was amazing to see this soothing couple's four hands wash, cut, comb, spray, pat. They were a flight of birds. With scissors in their hands they were storks. With spray bottles, puffins. With brushes, owls. With shampoo, cockatoos.

They nested their fat breasts on her head until it hatched.

The cracks in the shell were runny, dripping, and the being that came out was huge-eyed and soft-beaked with skin as thin as mist and down upon its skull. It was her, this thing above the smock. Her.

She loved herself.

The high walls of the valley collapsed in her chest with a soft rumble of feathers. Hal and the car and the fire and the thud disappeared in this thick, weightless cataract.

Of course they wouldn't accept any money. Instead, they said she could pay them by coming to their house for dinner. And Hal should come, too. But he wouldn't. He'd stay right where he was in this dreary hotel until the insurance man called. Fact was, he said, he couldn't stand to look at her and her awful haircut, much less the people who gave it to her.

So she went alone, her wings as light as wax paper, her twiggy legs wobbling, her eyes the size of the world.

GUIDEBOOK

Christopher Merrill

Erosion is the greatest threat to the stability of this island. Once as large as the imagination itself (galaxies, universes), now it fits snugly in the palm of your hand, its coastline having been eaten away by tides of a mysterious origin. Yet the population is exploding, and with shortages of food, water, and housing the clerics' prohibitions against contraception only anger the dispossessed—to say nothing of their edicts on the future of complex numbers and natural history, which frighten the elites, bewilder the scribes, and comfort the families of the sick and dying.

To quell the unrest, the authorities have created a bureaucracy to chart the weather, employing a sizable portion of the work force. Equipped with thermometers and wind vanes, field-workers fan out across the island at daybreak and do not return until dusk.

They send back hourly readings to statisticians who record and interpret their findings, which are broadcast everywhere; scrutinized by scholars, these statistics are the source of continuous debate. For time, like the coastline, has also shrunk, causing the seasons to change without warning; every solstice and equinox, of which there are more than a dozen a day, must be accounted for; the work is endless.

Scientists cannot determine if the weather and corresponding tides are a function of the planet tilting in a new direction, of a change in the orbit of the moon, or of fallout from a secret military experiment gone awry. How to account for the sudden emergence of spring after a summer-like drought—the new shoots sprouting in the cracks of the sidewalk, the erratic behavior of the swans circling the pond in the last park, the river overflowing its banks? Why is the autumnal division of fruits certain to succeed any shift in domestic or foreign policy? And where does winter figure into the calculations of the media, which have reaped enormous profits from the crisis?

Thus from hour to hour the road crews do not know whether they will need to repair potholes or plow snow; commercial jets stay in holding patterns all day long; the inversion never lifts. And the clerics? They have enlisted the homeless to keep track of who does what, when, and where. You, for example. Where are you supposed to be now? Why are you still here?

TEST

G. A. Ingersoll

Part One: Word Problems

Instructions: You have thirty minutes for this section. Record your answers legibly in the space provided. To be eligible for partial credit, be sure to show all of your work.

A) Leonard walks down aisle five at Price Chopper. He is eighty-six years old. He wears a size thirteen shoe. He puts the following items into the basket of his shopping cart: three cans of split pea soup, three cans of tomato soup, one can of chicken noodle soup. The price of each can is more than twice what it was four decades ago. Already in his cart are two boxes of oyster crackers (buy one get one free) and a package of all-beef hot dogs, for which he has a coupon for thirty-five cents. When his wife Rosa was dying of breast cancer, she made him swear to eat at least one hot meal a day. Rosa died three years ago this Sunday. Allowing for holidays with his married niece and the occasional church supper, how many cans of soup has Leonard consumed during this time period?

B) John and Linda meet at an AA meeting. John is twenty-three years old, and has been sober one year, three weeks, and two days. He lives in a rented rehearsal space, where he practices classical guitar and writes songs about isolation and longing. Linda is twenty-two years old, and has been clean forty-five days. She lives in a halfway house, where she practices not killing herself and writes in a recovery journal. He pursues her with melancholy poetry about beauty and sin, death and salvation. They become lovers, against the advice of her support group. They share a mutual kindness, an appreciation for modern European novelists, and a restlessness that each hopes will be satiated by enough restaurant food. John's depression deepens, although he is taking sixty milligrams daily of a popular antidepressant. Soon he can only lie on his bed and cry. He refuses to see anyone but Linda. After six weeks of this Linda breaks it off, fearing for her own stability. Six months later, John is dead of a heroin overdose. What should Linda say to his parents at the funeral?

C) Margaret's conscious death anxiety is such that she spends a total of thirty minutes daily obsessed with thoughts of dying prematurely. It has been shown that stress and anxiety contribute to heart disease, and heart disease is an up-and-comer as a killer of women. By how many years will Margaret's life be shortened by her fear?

D) Prudence is thirty-four. She has had sex with twenty-one men and three women. After being celibate for three years, she meets Larry and a romance begins to develop. Larry is thirty-seven. One night he proposes that, things going the way he thinks they're going between them, they talk about their sexual histories. Larry confesses to having slept with three women, one of whom he married. She tells him that she has slept with three men. Larry is uncomfortable with this number, especially since Prudence is younger than he is. She amends it, saying that one was just heavy petting. Given Prudence's reflexive need for approval and Larry's clear ideas of how things should be, what percentage of the time will Prudence be inhibited in bed with Larry, and consequently fake orgasm to ease his pride?

Part Two: Matching

Instructions: You have fifteen minutes for this section. Provide matches to the words in the left-hand column. Some of these words may have more than one match, so be sure to choose the best answer. Some of the words on the right may be used more than once, and some not at all.

A. Panic	1. Trouble
B. Routine	2. Normalize
C. Lucid	3. Soothe
D. Potential	4. Television

E. Rivalry	5. Grief
F. Prescription	6. Minimize
G. Isolation	7. Touch
H. Hunger	8. Alert
I. Shame	9. Imbalance
J. Ambition	10. Ache
K. Comfort	11. Compulsion
L. Methadone	12. Compliance
M. Prayer	13. Maladaptive

Part Three: Short Answer

Instructions: You have five minutes. Complete the statements by inserting the correct words or phrases in the parentheses.

A. ( ) makes the world go 'round.
B. Life is but a ( ).
C. It is ( ) fault.
D. People are ( ).
E. I wish I had never ( ).

Part Four: Essay

Instructions: You have thirty minutes for this section. Using the method of rational argumentation, answer each of the following questions and defend your position.

A. What is the genesis of pathology?
B. Why do you belong here?
C. Can you reconcile your desires with the needs of other people?

D. Assign a point value to each of your personal values. Determine which of these you can live without, and why.

Extra Credit

Fully explain the ways in which you are wrong.

DRAWER

Rick Moody

She called it an *armoire*, which was the problem, which was why he had dragged it onto the beach behind the house, and surveyed its progress over the course of a week, the elements driving down their varieties upon her *armoire*, their drama of erosion upon her *armoire*, a winter of steady rain, and had she been willing to call the *armoire* a *chest of drawers* like anybody else maybe they never would have arrived at this moment, or maybe *he* would never have arrived at this moment, he would not have found himself on the deck, in the rain, overlooking the beach, overlooking the *armoire* buried in sand up to the bottommost drawer (the work of tides), strands of kelp like accessories arranged around it, gray driftwood, lobster buoys, a Clorox bottle, a red plastic shovel, the pink detached arm of a chubby doll, plovers piping

there, alone on the wet deck with a stiff drink despite the newness
of the day, with a Sears deluxe crowbar with lifetime warranty he
intended to use on the *armoire*, if you want to know the goddamned truth, specifically the top drawer of the *armoire*, which
was locked now as it had always been locked in his presence,
though when they bought the imitation *18th century, Sheraton-
style armoire* at a flea market in the city, it hadn't bothered him
then that the drawer was locked and that she had taken control of
the little antique key, with its pair of teeth, *Anyone should have
been able to pick that goddamned lock*, open that drawer, and yet,
for all his accomplishments in the world of *franchise merchandis-
ing*, he couldn't do it, though maybe he had picked it and had forgotten, plenty to forget in these last few days, maybe he'd asked the
boys with the cooler and the Frisbee who'd chanced along the
shoreline, maybe he'd asked if they'd give a hand opening this
armoire, using her word when he said it, but they had backed away,
politely at first, then vehemently, into a temporarily radiant dusk,
even when he called after them, *Show a neighbor a little good
cheer! I got a thousand and one jokes!* Hadn't bothered him at first
that he had no key to her *armoire*, had no tongue to share the word
with her, the tongue which calls an *armoire* an *armoire*, not a
dresser, not a *chest of drawers*, as his father and his father had said
it, hadn't bothered him when the *armoire* was damaged in the *relo-
cation* to the seaside, *just a chip off the side, just a dent*, but she'd
gotten *apoplectic*, she'd taken photographs of the *armoire*, poorly
lit Polaroids, she'd called the dispatcher at the van lines *demand-
ing compensation*, though they had a hundred other pieces of furniture, deck chairs, poster beds, and a *joint bank account*, and she
had her own room to work in (painted a stifling blue), and he'd left
her alone, he'd walked upon the beach whistling lullabies, but
he'd never learned how to say the word *armoire* with any convic-
tion at all, and he would have included *demitasse* and *taffeta* and

sconce and *minuet*, actually, he'd gone gray trying to learn all these words, he'd become an *old unteachable dog* trying to learn how to say these things, how to say *I love you* he supposed, an isolated backyard hound in bare feet upon the coastal sand the goodly heft of a crowbar and the way wood gives under such an attack he would burn the damned thing plank by plank and heat the house with the past tense of her, would burn her diaries, leaf by leaf, in the *antique potbelly stove*, weather descriptions, breezy accounts of society functions, he would consume her secrets and her reserve so hidden as to be hidden even from herself, Lord, these people who never gave a goddamned thing.

00:02:36:58

Bayard Godsave

This was when LaSalle and I were somewhere between our childhood and our teens. It started with a video camera, a packet of contraband fireworks, and his pellet gun—one of those CO_2-powered things, a convincing facsimile of a .38 Smith & Wesson. LaSalle's sister would run the camera, I would be the gunman, and LaSalle would be the victim.

First, to LaSalle's stomach we taped this tin tray that his mom kept in their kitchen, where she threw her car keys and spare change when she got home from work; then to the tray we taped a bundle of Black Cats with their wicks twisted together; over this we taped a Ziploc baggie full of catsup—this last part was my idea.

"This'll never work," LaSalle said. "How am I going to get them lit?"

"We'll cut a hole," I said.

"In my shirt?"

"Yeah," I said. "In your shirt."

It was windy, and LaSalle did have trouble getting the wicks to catch. You can see it on the video, shaky and shot through the sub-shop window—where LaSalle's sister stood so that onlookers would not be aware of her presence, so that the whole thing wouldn't look like a hoax. We're out on the sidewalk, LaSalle and me, and LaSalle's hunched over, his back to the camera so you can't see what he's doing. We hadn't planned on this, him having trouble that is, so I had to improvise, to think of what I might say if I actually *did* want to shoot LaSalle. You can just barely hear me over the din of conversation in the sub shop. "Come on mother-fucker, turn around! Don't make me shoot you in the back!" Then LaSalle turns. I figured they would go off one at a time, the Black Cats, but instead they went off all together. You can see this too on the video, how I jerk the gun three times for the imagined recoil, despite there being only one pop, only one flash. And then the red spatter on LaSalle's tee shirt, LaSalle going down, me running off camera. And here's the best part: LaSalle's sister, inside the sub shop, is going, "Oh, shit. Oh, shit." And the conversation behind her has stopped. She pans upward. Across the street the lunch crowd outside the Bronze Bear Café is scrambling out from under their umbrellaed tables. They point. They wear expressions of dis-belief, expressions that say, This doesn't happen in our town. This doesn't happen.

Whenever I watch the tape, I find I can't help but pause it on this final moment. I stare at them there in freeze-frame. They're all standing, or in the midst of standing. The picture is grainy, and at that distance their mouths are little more than specks, black and vacuous in their blurred and anonymous faces. In only seconds they'll see LaSalle get up, a grinning Lazarus, and run off, disappearing somewhere down Main Street. But now, they are convinced. Now they only know that they are experiencing this very moment, that something horrible has happened, that they are each of them witness to something deeply tragic. And I'm reluctant to let the tape play on. I want to hold, in some continual present, this moment of cheap immortality, this one instant where me, and LaSalle, and LaSalle's kid sister made them long for everything to be right again with the world.

THE GOOD LIFE

David Ryan

Once, in San Diego, I was picked up at the airport by a woman I used to know in high school. She hadn't actually come for me, but had just flown in herself and recognized me standing at the baggage claim. *I thought it was you,* she said. I had never known her well—we'd kept with different circles—and so the enthusiasm of her embrace seemed misplaced. I recalled that her first name was almost the same as her last name. She offered to drive me to my hotel, then suggested dinner as we located her expensive car in the lot. She said she was in sales and was returning from a trip to Canada. She appeared to have done well. She drove too fast, and when her car took turns the tires sounded in a fine-tuned German shriek.

It was like old times without really having had any. As she

spoke, her thoughts seemed to arrive, light, and pass me in clusters of knotted logic, operating on some set of predetermined rules I hadn't learned, but liked the sound of anyway. *You've lost weight,* she said. *Imagine, you and me escaping that shit-hole.* At dinner she ordered glass after glass of wine and somehow remained sober, recalled things that happened to me that had never occurred, people we both knew well whom I hadn't known at all.

It eventually dawned on me that she had mistaken me for someone else. *Congratulations!* she said, toasting. Later, in the car, she turned off the air conditioning, took out a plastic bag filled with white powder, and held it out like a dead offering. *Pharmaceutical grade,* she said. *We take the money up to Vancouver,* she said. *The old rinse and spin. Cut it up like wedding cake.* I saw a man standing in the parking lot and recalled the name of a boy in high school who looked like me. We were seldom confused with each other, but then again years had passed. *My husband broke my back in two places,* she was saying. The man in the parking lot walked toward us, passed, and disappeared inside the door of another car. *Did you worry?* she said. She had stopped looking at me as she spoke. I no longer understood who she was talking to. *You know you've achieved peace when . . . ,* she began to say, but didn't finish. I could see where her nose had been broken, a small crest at the bridge the dark brought out. As if she realized I had noticed this, she lifted her face from the plastic bag, and said: *You get to where all you can see are the spaces between people passing on the street.*

FRUIT SERIES

Opal Palmer Adisa

Guava

The green exterior disguises perfectly the sweet pink-seeded meat that lives inside. This, her father told her, was a metaphor for how she was to dress, modestly, to hide the lascivious curves of her behind, as he was not able to protect or be with her all the time.

Breadfruit

Long ago, the god of the Taino people appeared to a guileless maiden and convinced her to allow him to sleep in her bed. The next morning she woke with a round-mounded stomach, and as she squatted in pain, the fruit spilled from her and fed the entire tribe.

Tamarind

Old age is said to be better than fortune, but she didn't agree. Left all day on the veranda, she wished she could be of use. Once, she knew which flowers were medicine and which could sweeten a pot, but now her fingers betrayed her with their stiff numbness.

Papaya

He always looked at a woman's mouth first. The shape told a lot, not just about kissing, but more, about how readily she would agree with him. Her mouth told him she was malleable; she would be good to the touch and someone worth savoring, all orange and black.

Mango

He tasted the sticky juice the moment his tongue licked her breast, and he was immediately transported to Bombay, a place he did not care to remember, where, many days as a boy, all he had to eat was the fruit he stole from a tree in someone's yard.

June-Plum

Raised as he was by a mother who whipped him when frustrated, he had scars on his back and legs as proof. Still, many thought him artless to ignore such a beautiful woman who spoke gently and smiled radiantly. But he said nothing, having eaten many june-plums as a child.

Guinep

They clung to each other fiercely, vowing never to be separated, but what did they know about how time and circumstances could erode the most spirited friendship. And, after college, the distance and demands of their careers led them down different paths until the phone calls dwindled to special occasions.

Naseberry

He had been craving something sugary when he saw her in the ice cream store wearing a yellow silk dress that shimmered when she moved. He couldn't decide which flavor to order so asked her, as an opening line. She looked at him, smiled demurely, said: "Me, I'm incredibly sweet."

Otaheite Apple

Her scarlet skirt hid the purity of her heart. True, she flirted, but it was all a guise. Her innocence was fleshy white, but in his terror to possess her, to break her spirit, he bit into her, his rage covering her screams, and her ribbons fell limply.

INITIALS ETCHED ON A DINING-ROOM TABLE, LOCKEPORT, NOVA SCOTIA

Peter Orner

The girl was young when she did it, and she didn't live there. This was in 1962. She was eighteen. She'd been hired to tidy the place. It was three, maybe four years before anybody noticed. The letters were so small, and they always ate in the kitchen. And when they did discover them, she was already gone to Halifax. By that time the girl had a reputation to escape from. So when they put two and two together and figured out it was she that did it, they weren't surprised. Of course she'd be the one to do something like this, they said—shameless girl, not shocking at all.

A cod fisherman, a captain, lived in the house with his wife, one of the original Locke mansions on Gurden Street overlooking the harbor. They never had children, but dust collects nonetheless in a house so huge. The girl had never been in a place that grand. At least that's what they told each other when they found her letters. *RGL.* That she'd wanted to leave her mark in the world, something that would last, something that would stay. The family still lived in town, her father and brothers sold hardware, so they could have held somebody accountable for the damage if they'd wanted to. But the captain and his wife talked it over and decided not to mention it to anyone. Not that they approved—Lord no. It was defacement of property. Vandalism. Of course it was an heirloom; it had belonged to her mother's mother, a burnished mahogany drop-leaf built in York in 1844. They could never approve. But they were quiet people; they kept to themselves in the hard times, and even in the good times they held their distance. Besides, what could anybody do about it now? What was done was done. Still, that didn't mean the captain's wife didn't watch more carefully over the other girls who came to clean, and it didn't mean the captain didn't sometimes think of her sugar breath, that morning, the one out of a thousand when he was home and slept late—he'd startled her in the kitchen. *Captain Adelbert! I didn't have any idea you were home, me banging the pots down here to wake the dead.* His only intention was to touch her sweater (Lucy was out, still teaching school then), but he couldn't stop and kissed her, her hands at her sides. She didn't resist or desire, and that had made him a fool for years.

YET OVER THE LONGER YEARS—when the fish became scarcer, when they'd long since failed their vow to fill that house with children, when the silences between them sometimes lasted hours, when the captain's wife no longer paced the house, waiting for him, or word of him—an odd thing. They still talked about the letters. *RGL* became a part of the table that had always been too good to eat on, as important as the deep swirls carved at the top of the legs. She. The simple fact of her once among them, among their things, dusting, opening closet doors, tracing her finger along the frames of the paintings in the front room. Taking a needle—she must have used a needle—and climbing up on the table, walking *on* her knees to a spot just off the center.

In the dark, now older, now retired, still in the house, they murmur: "She was a pretty girl, wasn't she?"

"Curls. Yes, yes. Got in trouble with the boys early on, didn't she?"

"What do you think the G stands for?"

"Gina? Gertrude?"

"Georgette?"

"Never came back here ever."

"No, never heard of it. Family acts like she never existed."

"Well. She was a disgrace, I suppose."

"Yes, well."

They both think of her. Sleep comes slowly. Now the captain coughs and twists. Age and too much time on land have made him restless, a man who was never restless, a man who had always slept the unmovable sleep of beached whales, now tossing and muttering, waking with sweat-wet hands, afraid. Now he dreams of drowning. And the captain's wife stares at the ceiling in the dark and thinks of leading a child, Rachel Larsh's child, an angry boy in new leather shoes, through the house, pointing out the captain's trophies, the swordfish he caught during that trip to the Pacific (on the wall in the library), the hidden staircase behind the summer kitchen, and here, see, look, beneath the vase he brought back from St. John, your mother's initials. And the boy not curious, shaking free his hand.

MR. NIKOS NIKOU

Ersi Sotiropoulos

translated from the Greek by Stratis Haviaras

I fear for my mother. I fear that my mother is being tortured by something terrible, but I don't know what. This something has to do with me. A certain Mr. Nikos Nikou has been visiting with us quite often lately. My mother receives him without any formality whatever. When I go to the kitchen to announce that he's arrived and he's waiting for her in the dining room, she feigns dismay. She wipes her hands and proceeds to meet him without taking off her apron.

They lock themselves in that room for about half an hour each time. I have the impression that my mother talks the whole time. Mr. Nikou just listens, never interrupting. I wait in a chair in the corridor, with my fingers in my ears. Without intending to, every once in a while I make out some words: "The boy! . . . The boy! . . ." She repeats. Her voice rises, full of anguish.

My mother is afraid of me. There are times when she looks at me as though she sees me for the first time. At the start she appears rather absentminded, then gradually her face assumes an expression of panic, which now she doesn't even try to hide. At other times I sense her staring at my back and I suddenly turn around. She is standing in the middle of the room. She is pale, paralyzed with fear. The pupils of her eyes, dilated and still like those of a fish, pin me down without a trace of motherly affection. From time to time I get carried away and attempt a couple of steps toward her. She then runs straight to her room. She locks herself in and bursts into tears.

Usually I am the first one to leave the scene. I go to my room and lie down waiting for the night. The hours pass, the traffic in the street thins. With the lights turned off I follow the reflected patterns that begin at the blinds, cross the ceiling swiftly, and vanish at the corners of the walls.

I DREAMED THAT MR. NIKOS NIKOU loved me very much and wanted to take me with him. Flowers grew everywhere in his house. Through the floor there sprouted roses with thick stems among chrysanthemums and bougainvilleas. I walked in a corridor full of weeds and went to his room. His bed was a flat planter covered with yellow tulips.

I felt awfully tired and lay down. The flowers moved softly under my weight, and as I sank horizontally, it began to get dark. With tender strokes the tendrils coiled around my body. Yet I was not afraid. The smell of the soil, strong like fresh-baked bread, hit my nostrils as the earth was pulling me deeper. Farther on I saw my mother on a bed of violets, also being sucked in, smiling.

THREE SOLDIERS

Bruce Holland Rogers

1. The Hardest Question

My marines bring me questions. "When do we get to shower?" "Sergeant, how do you say 'Good afternoon' again?" "Sarge, where can I get more gun oil?"

I have answers. "Tomorrow, maybe." *"Maysuh alheer."* "Use mine."

Answering their questions is my job. But when Anaya was shot and bleeding out, he grabbed my arm and said, "Sergeant? Sergeant?" I understood the question, but damn. I didn't have an answer.

2. Foreign War

No U.S. soldier who could see that kid would have shot him. But that's long-range ordnance for you. Calder stood next to me in the street, looking at the pieces. "We've come so far from home," he said, "that we'll never get back."

"You dumbass," I said. But a year later I stood on the tarmac hugging my child, thinking of that kid in pieces, and I wasn't home.

3. Decisions, Decisions

In morning twilight, far away, my men are making up their minds:
> What's that guy carrying?
> Friend or foe?

I should be there, helping them decide. My wife and my parents do their best to make Christmas dinner conversation around my silence. An hour ago, I was yelling at Angie for turning on the damn news. My father, carving, won't meet my eyes. He says, "White meat, or dark?"

THE MESMERIST

Michael Knight

Moody boarded the Silver Star bound for DC, where he would hop the Crescent and ride it through the night. There was a dinner theater in New Orleans looking for a mesmerist to open the show, and he had played well there in the past. In the seat opposite his, a girl was reading a fashion magazine. She was wearing a sweatshirt (BOSTON UNIVERSITY CHAMBER MUSIC SOCIETY), and every few seconds she tucked the same wayward strand of hair behind her ear. Moody had a gift for reading people and, in this girl, he recognized a sadness, something familiar and close to his heart. He saw it in the slump of her shoulders. He saw it in the hint of wear and tear around her eyes. She was hopeful and afraid. She had been unlucky all her life. This girl would have a broken heart before too long.

"Are you watching me?" she said. "I hate being watched."

She closed the magazine and leveled a glare at Moody. In one motion, he reached into the pocket of his coat, withdrew a penlight, and flicked the beam across her line of sight. He said, "Every muscle in your body is limp now. I am pulling your eyes closed with silken threads." The girl opened her mouth, but instead of speaking, she slumped in her seat. He counted down from ten to one, and when he was finished, she was perfectly asleep. Her hands upturned and pendulous beside her. Her head bobbing as they rocked across a trestle. She looked vaguely surprised.

IN PHILADELPHIA, MOODY steered her along the tide of exiting passengers. He bought a pair of tickets in a sleeping berth to Cleveland. While they rolled cross-country in the dark, Moody described the life they would have together. He said she would never be lonely. He told her she would be possessed of grace and charm. "I'm going to count again," he said. "This time, when you wake, you will no longer be acquainted with unhappiness."

MOODY FOUND DAY WORK and they rented in a neighborhood sumptuous with brick and shade. They were happy for a while. Penelope took piano lessons from an elderly woman on the block, Mrs. Berryman, who often stopped Moody on the street and said, "That Penelope of yours is the most confident beginner I've ever had. It's like she knows piano in her bones." If the weather was right for open windows, Moody could hear her practicing when he walked home at night. He would stand in the yard marveling at the simple bricks and elegant maples and surprise himself with the notion that this was the life he had been looking for all his days.

ONE EVENING, ALREADY within earshot of Penelope's piano, Moody spotted a stranger peeking in the windows. It was fall, leaves chameleoning on their branches. Moody hurried up the street, calling a friendly hello, wondered aloud what the man was doing on his porch. The man smiled in what Moody guessed was meant to be a reassuring way.

"I'm a private investigator," he said. "I've been looking for a girl." He retrieved a photograph from his briefcase—Penelope with a green ribbon pinned to her shoulder.

"What did she win?" Moody said.

"Second prize in the Fairfax County Piano Recital," he said. "She did Chopin. Her name's Penelope."

Moody slipped his penlight from his pocket, flicked the beam in his practiced manner. He lowered his voice and said, "You have made a mistake. There is no Penelope here."

"I have made a mistake," the man repeated. "There is no Penelope here."

His eyes were glazed, his mouth hanging open. The photograph fluttered from his fingertips.

Moody said, "Perhaps she has run off to Honduras. You should go down and have a look."

"Perhaps she has run off to Honduras," the man said. "I should go down and have a look."

Moody watched him stagger up the sidewalk to his car and drive away. He bent and picked up the picture, stood looking at it until Penelope's music came back to him, a melancholy sound on the fragile air.

AT CHRISTMAS, THEY invited lonely Mrs. Berryman over and after dinner she sat beside Penelope on the piano bench and they played duets of holiday songs. When she was tired, they bundled Mrs. Berryman into her coat and walked her home. They stood at the curb and watched the snow gathering on the hood of Moody's car.

Penelope said, "I love how the snow muffles and magnifies everything at the same time. My voice sounds so loud just now."

Moody slipped his arm around her waist, let the deepening silence drift back in behind her words. He kissed the top of Penelope's head, her hair cold and brittle and dusted with snow.

He said, "You should have worn your hat."

"I'll be fine," she said. "You mother me too much, Moody."

She leaned her head on his shoulder and drew him against her. Christmas trees shone through parted curtains. The snow sparkled. Moody wondered if their footprints would be covered by morning.

TOASTERS

Pamela Painter

The neighbors are at it again is what Joey says, just what his father would say if he were here. And just like his father, Joey shuts off all the lights, peels back the curtains over the sink, and settles in to watch the show.

The kitchen table is piled high with hot, dry laundry. I can fold it in the dark so I sit here listening to Joey describe what is flying out the Angelos' windows. So far it's plates, clothes, poker chips, and a fishing rod.

"Jesus, Mom, you're missing it. Mr. Angelo threw out the toaster. Wait'll Dad hears that." His excited sneakers thump the stove as he turns to ask if I remember when Mrs. Angelo flattened a whole row of my tomato plants with a bowling ball.

I tell him it's way past bedtime but he just gets his nose closer

216

to the window to identify the next object and assess the damage. They keep lists—Joey and his father. Things thrown, sound effects made, and grievances screamed to the heavens as if to bring down a pre-apocalyptic condemnation.

Tonight it started with Mrs. Angelo's mother's weekend visits and moved on to Mr. Angelo's unfinished basement projects and early exits from his weekly poker game to parts and/or parties unknown. It is the same game my Harry has been losing too much money in for years and getting worse. The threadbare towels I'm folding are thin as silk and fold as flat.

"Wow," Joey says as Mrs. Angelo yowls one of her favorite four-letter words and the names of two forgiving saints. On purpose, I'm mismatching Harry's socks and thinking the exact same thing as Mrs. Angelo.

"Mom," Joey says, getting tired of the Angelos' show. "Where's Dad? Why isn't he home?"

Tonight I'll have to tell him. Because me and Harry. We're at it again too.

The streetlight from Joey's window glints on our toaster, plugged in and safe, and I think: me and Harry should take lessons from the Angelos. I admire the way they fight—everything flying out the windows and doors except the two of them.

DIAGNOSTIC DRIFT

Michael Martone

1.

You flowed and flowed. You stood in the bathtub, the blood sheeting your legs. I called the doctor who said to bring you in and who later said there were probably always this many miscarriages. He was speaking of the general population, not you. Back then, he said, they were mistaken for menstrual bleeding. These days new tests let us know sooner. We call this diagnostic drift, he said, a condition always present but unseen. Until now. Now we know what we are seeing sooner. You had held your dress up away from the blood, and I had daubed at your bleeding with a wet washcloth. You hadn't known you were pregnant until you weren't. A classic case, the doctor said. Should we worry, I asked. Should this have happened? It is diagnostic drift, the doctor said. A few years ago you wouldn't even know what happened happened. This happens all the time. We won't even need to notice until the third time it happens, if it even happens again at all.

2.

There there, another doctor said. It happens all the time. This time, you had known earlier you were pregnant and had been pregnant longer. Later, you'd seen a sign, you said, the day it happened. An English sparrow chick dead on the sidewalk you walked on the way home. In the bathtub, the blood was thicker this time and there was tissue in the pile of the washcloth. The doctor asked us to bring it in with us to the emergency room. There, there, she said. It is difficult, the doctor said. She held your hand. This happens all the time. There is no way of knowing. We know more now, she said, but we don't know everything. We'll keep an eye on it, she said, riffling through the sheets of paper. You looked off into the distance. At a distance, I looked at you, your hair fanned out on the white paper sheet.

3.

It is more common than you might think, this doctor said to me. You were getting dressed behind the curtain. You had started bleeding during a prenatal visit. Things had been going well this time. Your doctor called me at work. He wanted me to drive you to the hospital, didn't want you to drive yourself. She's lost some blood, he said. She's a bit light-headed, he said to me on the phone. I drove through the streets of a new city. We had just moved. All the streets looked the same: three flats and cyclone-fenced front yards. It was the doctor at the hospital who said that this was more common than you'd think. While you were there, I walked around the blocks of hospital buildings. I walked around three times. I told the doctor about the other times, about the doctor who had told us of diagnostic drift and that now we should be paying attention. Let's just wait and see, she said. These things happen. I asked her how long we should wait before we tried again, and she thought, for some reason, I meant exercise instead of sex. As soon as possible, she said. The sooner the better. But then when she understood what I had meant she said, oh that. I watched your shadow move on the white cloth screen. Give it a few days, weeks, a month or so, maybe. Talk with your doctor.

4.

There is no blood. There's nothing to be done. There is your heartbeat but the other one is gone. The doctor has his nurse make the arrangements at a clinic for the D&C. We know the city better now. The main roads empty into rotaries I must circle, working my way around to the new road I need to take. I drop you off at the clinic. There is no place to park, so I idle at the front gate. You're escorted in through the picket of a few silent protesters. I drive around the city, lazily circling the rotaries a few times, and then cruise along the highway next to the widening river where eights and fours skate back and forth on the smooth surface, disappearing in the shadows beneath the old bridges. I know we know more now than we did but it is hard to say. I know right now you are being questioned. An aide is asking questions and writing your answers onto forms she keeps in a file. Your history is being worked up. This happened and this happened and this happened and then this.

YOU DON'T KNOW ANYTHING

Kathleen Wheaton

"Poor things," my mother murmured, hurrying me past the docks in Buenos Aires, where brown, wiry boys hoisted gunnysacks and shouted to each other in Sicilian.

"Why don't they go to school?"

"Well, my love, they're immigrants."

As if *we* weren't. But we didn't think of ourselves that way. My father had managed to persuade my mother, pregnant with me, to get on a boat for Argentina in the nick of time. She and I waited for him, and finally stopped waiting, in an apartment on Calle Bolívar, opposite a pastry shop. I was a fat boy, who wept over minor disappointments, and these two facts represented my mother's personal victory over the Nazis.

In Buenos Aires, you didn't hear German on the street. Jews avoided it because it had been Hitler's language; the others from our country, laying low, for the same reason. I believed, when I was small, that my mother had made it up. By the time I was in school, it was simply the language of reprimand.

I brought a girl to the apartment on Bolívar when I was sixteen. My mother was out, giving a piano lesson, a detail I didn't reveal to Leticia until we were standing in our kitchen, which, I noticed for the first time, smelled of boiled milk and laundry.

"So? I'm not exactly afraid of you." Leticia flipped her dark hair over her shoulder. She was one of the first to wear it long and straight.

I showed her the black-and-white photographs which were the pretext for her visit. They were pictures I'd taken along Avenida de Mayo, shot from angles that made my subjects loom ominously: a pigeon, a discarded newspaper, striding trouser legs.

"Good, good," Leticia said, nodding as she thumbed through them, like a policeman checking documents. She was known at school as *artistica*, a broad-spectrum word that contained the rumor that she'd slept with a university student.

I'd considered various ways the conversation might go once she'd approved the pictures. "Do you think you'd go to bed with me?" I heard myself say.

Leticia burst out laughing. "Do you mean now, or in theory?"

The only possible thing was to act as though my question hadn't been a monstrous error. "Now," I said firmly, though my cheeks burned as she stared at me. I'd imagined inspecting Leticia, of course, but in these daydreams I was invisible. I was shambling, bearlike; some years later I'd luck into a resemblance to Gérard Depardieu. But at that time, I suppose, he was an unknown French kid, also hoping to get laid.

I glanced at the clock over the door, where my mother had hung it when I started *preparatoria*, to encourage punctuality. "Never mind," I said. "The piano lesson finishes in half an hour."

"You don't know anything, do you?" Leticia said, smiling. She seemed to find the danger of the situation exciting. One minute before the bus would have stopped on the corner of Avenida Belgrano, we were back at the kitchen table, dressed and posed with the photo album. My mother walked in and greeted my new love politely, asked if she'd prefer tea or *mate*. As she turned to light the flame under the kettle, she said softly, "I'm sorry you're reduced to having sluts for friends, Peter."

Horrified, I turned to Leticia. The dark eyes I'd thought twenty minutes ago I was falling into were opaque; the smile on her pretty red lips didn't fade. She doesn't know German, I thought. She doesn't know anything, I thought. "Poor thing," I said.

TRAVELING ALONE

Rob Carney

Maybe it's different when you grow up around lightning. Say if you're from Kansas where all it is, is normal. Normal and dangerous, and you know exactly what it's like to catch the whipcrack end of the stuff with your roof, or barn, or with the only tree around for miles. But that's not me. To me, it's incredible. I mean, I look forward to it when it smells like lightning's coming. When it slashes and streaks and you can hear it sizzling apart the night. I totally love that. So guess what: I was on a plane one time—this was about three years ago—a little puddle jumper out of Dallas down to Lake Charles—so we must've been over East Texas or Shreveport—it could've been Arkansas—wherever—the point is, out the window was this giant cloud that looked like a lightning *factory*. You know, I mean, you should've seen it. It wasn't shooting out lightning bolts. They were all happening *inside* the cloud, so these areas would suddenly flash in the middle . . . then somewhere else . . . then *pmm pmm pmm pmm pmm* all in a row . . . like if you were standing outside a welding shop in the dark, in the snow, and seeing all these blue-white flashes through windows covered in dust. Sort of like that. And it just went on and on and on not stopping. And, I mean, it really did look like a factory. You know, like this was where and how lightning was made, then shipped around the world to thunderstorms. Like down there in the middle, gods were working with hammers and anvils and bellows and wearing those helmets with a little strip of glass to look out of. Like a cloudy furnace. Like the birthplace of light. Like maybe that's the way the universe looked in the womb. God, I wished someone would've been there with me. It was the kind of thing that's twice as good to share.

THE DEATH OF THE SHORT STORY

J. David Stevens

The Story's death caught us all off guard. We'd been watching Poetry so closely that we failed to heed the warning signs. One day the Story was here, watching football, going to singles bars, making quiche. The next day—POOF!—we were reading about his demise in the *Times*, our bagels forgotten, our untouched lattes forming white rings on the dark wood of our kitchen tables.

Naturally there was a public outcry. On TV, we watched the crowds stack flowers and stuffed animals outside libraries worldwide. Soon the talk shows buzzed with innuendo. A genre cut down in its prime, they claimed. Audiences were stunned when the Memoir admitted to an affair with the Story during her "repressed childhood memory" phase. Media scrutiny became so intense that the entire Autobiography family left town for a month to work out its issues in private.

At the funeral, the Prose Poem delivered a eulogy where she referred to publishers as "market whores" and called academics "literary vultures happier since the Story's departure." But in truth, we were all to blame. We milled around the reception feeling sheepish, thinking about what we might have done. In a corner, the loutish Novel got drunk on cheap Chardonnay and babbled about the good times he and the Story had shared. He consoled himself by hugging random passersby and saying "I Love You!" much too loudly for the comfort of the lit mag editors several feet away.

In the weeks that followed, rumors began to circulate about how the Story's brain had been cryogenically stored in a bunker near Omaha. A Glasgow professor offered a thousand pounds to anyone who could produce a sample of the Story's DNA, for cloning purposes. Still others maintained that the Story was not gone at all, but had faked his death and retired to an isolated mountain retreat in the Andes or the Himalayas.

This last idea redeemed us somehow. We began to make up lies about the Story, lies which seemed like truth after a while. We pictured the Story sitting around a fireplace with John Lennon, Jesus, and Amelia Earhart, where they sipped century-old cognac and talked about what players to put on their All-Time Fantasy Baseball Teams. They wore the socks that we'd lost in the dryer over the years and jangled the spare change that had dropped between our sofa cushions. A single bay window looked out over the mountains from which they could see, above the clouds, a spinning whirlpool of various colors. The colors, they imagined, were their dreams, and they waited patiently for those moments when a sliver of light would break loose from the oblong, suspended momentarily like a musical note on fire before streaking recklessly into the surrounding night.

CREDITS

Opal Palmer Adisa, "Fruit Series" was first published in ZYZZYVA 67 (Spring 2003). Reprinted by permission of the author.

Leonardo Alishan, "The Black City" is reprinted from the *Prairie Schooner* 78, no. 1 (Spring 2004), by permission of the University of Nebraska Press. Copyright © 2004 by the University of Nebraska Press.

Steve Almond, "Rumors of Myself" was first published in *StoryQuarterly* 39 (2003). Reprinted by permission of the author.

Cynthia Anderson, "Baker's Helper" was first published in *Iowa Review* 32, no. 1 (Spring 2003). Reprinted by permission of the author.

Michael Augustin, "The Handbag," translated by Sujata Bhatt, is reprinted by permission of the author and the translator.

DAVID RYAN, "The Good Life" was first published in *New Orleans Review* 29, no. 1 (2003). Reprinted by permission of the author.

SAMANTHA SCHOECH, "Why You Shouldn't Have Gone in the First Place" was first published in *On The Page* (Autumn 2001). Reprinted by permission of the author.

KEITH SCRIBNER, "Level" is reprinted with permission of Regal Literary as agent for Keith Scribner. Copyright © 2002 by Keith Scribner. Originally printed in *Quarterly West* (2002).

DON SHEA, "Jumper Down" was first published in *High Plains Literary Review* (1997). Reprinted by permission of the author.

ERSI SOTIROPOLOUS, "Mr. Nikos Nikou," translated by Stratis Haviaras, is reprinted by permission of the author and the translator.

J. DAVID STEVENS, "The Death of the Short Story" was first published in *The North American Review* (Nov.–Dec. 1998). Reprinted by permission of the author.

JAMES TATE, "Map of the Lost World" was first published in *New American Writing* 22 (2004). Reprinted by permission of the author.

PAUL THEROUX, "The Memory Priest of the Creech People" first appeared in *Harper's*, copyright © 1998 by Paul Theroux, reprinted with the permission of The Wylie Agency.

MELANIE RAE THON, "Blind Fish" was first published in *Colorado Review* 28 (Summer 2001). Reprinted by permission of the author.

ALISON TOWNSEND, "The Barbie Birthday" was first published in *The Blue Dress*, Buffalo, NY: White Pine Press (2003). Reprinted by permission of the author.